GABRIEL ZELDIS

iUniverse, Inc.
Bloomington

Fallen Angels

iUniverse books may be ordered through booksellers or by contacting:

iUniverse
1663 Liberty Drive
Bloomington, IN 47403
www.iuniverse.com
1-800-Authors (1-800-288-4677)

ISBN: 978-1-4502-6905-6 (sc)
ISBN: 978-1-4502-6906-3 (e)

Library of Congress Control Number: 2010918357

Printed in the United States of America

iUniverse rev. date: 12/2/2010

I left from Colorado, sometime during the afternoon. Although, I only made it five hours down the highway towards California. The place that could very well have been a place of miracles and dreams. The wind blowing down through the plains made it nearly impossible for me to drive the truck and trailer any farther west. I realized that things were changing, and I needed to make appropriations. Meaning the west which had been burning with wild fires and the red sun which the smoke hazed, was now becoming something to look at and learn from. The signs showed that times were changing and we as human beings and people had to keep vigil. I turned back to Colorado and drove up to the Rocky Mountains, up to a place called the Poudre Canyon which is in a State Forest area. I made a brief phone call and set myself up in a cabin above Indian Meadows and not yet to Chambers Lake. The winter then came and like time passed... There are many stories to tell, many stories to pull from. Life takes belief I guess and without it things aren't real like so many of these struggles. We live in a beautiful world, and with beautiful creatures and love around us. My story is dynamic. And the story of Fallen Angels is long.

What would be of our blue earth or our world, this vast world is hard to say. The snow fell in a barren winter. And the winds blew through the mountains; It was cold outside, very cold and it would get this way often. I would check my thermostat, to make sure the house could keep warm. And the snow would blow passed my windows. As far as I knew I had gone on in life, the past was over it was gone whatever it was. I don't really know, I'm not really sure. I have seen quite a bit, and I'm never quite sure. I had my eyes on California. I wanted to move out and make money in the Music Industry. And to make it in Hollywood. The east coast, was a step in the right direction, I like music and raves and I didn't know I had to convince the people in the industry to like music. I wasn't doing music therapy so I didn't know what to say, maybe stay away from the Hudson. Yes, and you all know it runs in upstate New York as well, the same Hudson. Wow, we all know the same things in life. We're all right there. Sure, whatever. Your movies are so awesome. Ok. So sometimes you have to ride the waves of hope and sometimes you walk with your board, I don't know why the waves aren't good sometimes. I just don't know. Couldn't tell you. It's just. Just. The west coast had potential, and so I thought getting lost in California would be a good thing.

I met the Black Angels under the fair skies of the Midwest. The sun shone as it usually does out there. And the beautiful river rolled...

The Pale heart of beauty. The violent waves. The crows that flew in the hours that past by the soloing guitars and the pink sunshine that shone. When the western sun reaches the sea the blazing maroon gem, the blazing maroon sun radiated and on new moons, new moons horizons where violets and white and violets catch the sun and the blue nights. Where the tiger lilies. Where white tigers dances in the sky. Where they spread their wings. The silver sun rays like glass, the melting stain glass. Sounds like the river bend, and the sky and the yellow sun. Wolves that might dance or cats that might dream in another world. This mango night, when will I ride the night train.

The burning violets, chilly with gold. Violets burn in fires. Of the sun set in gold. Unity and peace and unity and love the fires rage and the fires will rage in the light. I am myself and we who have flown on autumn winds, or on the cold kept the gold and river gold as in gold the fair blue skies. The cold and the air is cold. I have seen this town when the snow and ice fell. And when the sun is shining. I always hope for the future. I always hope we'll be in the hope-filled light dancing and alive. As God would have.

But I know being alive entails more than this. This dark and treacherous dream. And who is to say it's really happening it's not the poet that for you though fate and ivory are the colors of this dream, this dream that is more real than tomorrow. Is this real? This world or I'll think about it in time, the sun that is soon to rise is warm and real and there is more that is going on than I see . The black pearl sea, and the white crests. I see the black sea the forever changing tide the miracles and the things. The cold black sea and the pale blue sky, the paled heart of beauty, the paled heart of vivid beauty. We're alive but are changing like water and violets, and violets bleed, and violets bleed. The sun is violet, and violets bleed. The pansies dance, and the violets are alive.

History is a bleeding rose, and so when the cold hours pass...

My Downcast Eyes

Moonlight danced on the water.
Waves in their silence sung to my soul.
I envisioned the Lord holding me close as I wept.
What did I do to deserve this?
Why have you let me go, and to whom shall I turn?
For this is a desert I live in.
Love is scarce and soullessly we dwell.
I am taught not to trust, that faith is imaginary
And hope does not exist.
Only the hot sun, the flames, the fire.
There is no real shelter, only shade,
Only the shadow that I fear.
Where are you?
Where have you gone?
How can I trust in this chaos,
This madness that does not cease?
The clouds are dark overhead and
It rains inside my spirit.
What is this place I call home?
Could there really be a haven?
For I once believed and You seemed so real.
But this is a horrid land.
The memories are merely dreams.
That child I once was, this wretched man now I
Inlaid with shame, downcast and downtrodden.
Here we hold hands and carry one another off to sea.
A sea that is lifeless.
A sea that nothing runs out of.
A sea that has nothing in He.
Lord take me back to the deserted shores
Where I once lived, for there at least I can rest.

I was a prisoner then. I was a stranger in a world I could never understand, believing the things I did for it kept me sane, doing things I did not want to do; I could not help myself.

CHAPTER 1

By The Water's Edge

We walked by the water's edge. The lake was still, and the steam rose slowly from its surface. The trail we walked on was worn, and the roots of the tall evergreens stretched bare across our path. The fresh country air cared for the dew in sweet reverence and kissed the morning light hesitantly peering from above. The old mountains rolled taller here. Even the Hudson ran peaceful here, and her charm was enhanced by every curve. It was precious land, somehow still preserved. Its beauty was resting, and captured those who were within.

Every year my parents would take us up to this part of New York State, about twenty-six miles northwest of Still Water. And every year, we would rent an old cabin on a small, hidden lake, called Lake Trinity. I loved every minute of those times. I felt blessed to be able to spend those hours with my family. Those are the memories I have chosen to capture in my memory. I was just shy of eight years old.

I bent down to pick up my left sock that had been falling down. "Dumb quitter." "Wait up dad. Wait up!" My fishing rod shook, and my tackle box rattled. I ran impatiently down the old dusty way.

"How many are were going to catch today?" My dad was walking funny; he'd been drunk since the time I was born. " What do I look like dad," he responded. (My dad used to call me dad. I never knew why.) "Dad let's take that one," I pointed to a big green rowboat. "You gotta to be captain huh."

We clunked our way in and shoved off. Passed the green lily pads, and shallow water bottom. Passed the homemade dock, where a fake owl sat. We squeaked across the inlet with every pull of the oars.

" Dad where did you get your name?"

" My father, Thomas Francis senior."

" Dad, your middle name is Francis?"

" Don't make fun of your father." There was that look in his eyes I didn't want to see.

"Sorry, that's just a funny name. Francis? I can't believe it."

" Where were you born? Dad?" I asked just so he would speak with me.

" In Switzerland."

" Then how did you get here?"

" I left to see the world. I traveled to Bermuda and then to Italy. I moved to New York City and met your mother."

As I looked down through the clear water trying to spot some fish, I asked inquisitively: " What's Bermuda?"

" An island in the tropics." He didn't seem to care much about it.

"Oh, that's where you caught the electric eel and scared all the people with it right?"

" I didn't know it was poisonous. I brought it to the kitchen to cook for dinner, all the chefs ran away from me."

I started cracking up when I heard that, I thought it was so funny.

"Then what did you do? Did you chase them with it?"

"No. Someone finally told me what it was."

"Then what did you do? Did you throw it in a blender and splatter the guts everywhere?"

"No Josiah."

My dad rowed the squeaky boat to an even quieter part of the lake. That day we were going to a special fishing hole called Perch Cove. When we were about a stone's throw away, dad put the oars up and let the boat drift. I let the tip of my rod touch the surface of the water, and watched its wake tickle the stillness before us. Dad took the anchor we made from an old bleach container, and slowly let it down. No one else in the whole world knew what was inside that anchor except for dad and me: There was a layer of rock. Then pebbles. Then rock again. Then sand, two worms, and another level of pebbles. I stacked them right up to the blue cap. It was a really good anchor!

The murky bottom erupted as a mushroom cloud covered over the white container and bright yellow rope. I looked up at my dad with widened eyes of admiration. " This is a good spot, huh dad." My dad lit a cigarette and looked out across the cove. " It's fine."

The sun began to break through areas of the clouds where morning swallows dove from their heights and loved the water. They picked the strider bugs off the surface for breakfast. Nearby, a woman clunked a pair of shoes on her back porch. I heard the echoes.

Further down the shore, a couple loaded their belongings into a silver canoe. Yards away, an older man sat on an older dock, and pulled sunnies from below. And around this tattered edge, though gently carved with age, the tall pines made their way. I knew no other place which made me feel like I was home, as this place did.

Dad was preparing his line. He looped his womb, adjusted his bobber (so the womb would be closer to the bottom), and gave it a whirl. I watched his bobber and line fly in one direction. His worm, which separated from the hook, took route in the other direction. After making an unusually high arch, it fell about three yards away from me. I started to giggle and tugged at the back of my dad's shirt. " Dad you got to loop your worm more than once, the fish are going to get all full and we won't catch any."

I dug through the night crawler container and picked out a worm for each of us. We looped up together. I made sure to do my special, two and a half looper dooper, so no fish would steal my bait. My dad was preparing to cast, and so I hurried up to cast at the same time. By accident our lines tangled behind us. We looked out, each to a different area of the lake, expecting our bait to land. Clunk! Our bobbers smacked together on the metal boat bottom. "Oops," I said, and gave another little giggle.

Some of the most meaningful moments I have ever spent in my life were those I spent with my father fishing. I loved to spend time with him, although I wish it were as good for him, as it was for me. I always seemed to fumble up the "fishing experience." I think my tackle box might have been haunted. It must have been because I managed to mess up everything.

"Dad."

"What Josie."

"I did another knot."

"How do you do that?" He would say in a high voice.

I would get these knots in my line that always made casting a difficult chore. Without any given notice, without any warning sign, or slightest twinge of foreshadowing, when everything was going perfectly well indeed, a knot would catch and would send my friendly worm flying confidently through the air. Depending on the point of departure, the whip lashing, short stop could catapult my worm to unforeseen heights, or send him skipping across the water.

I remember one time my worm flew off and stuck to my dad's neck. I personally found it funny, although my dad didn't think it was so cute. Looking back, I wonder if it was really a bad cast, or if I just threw the worm at him.

It took years before I caught my first fish. One day at Cradle's Lake, I finally landed one. I was so excited afterwards I actually cast my reel off of my rod. (Don't ask.) I made mom go in and try to find it. She bravely inched around in the muck until the lifeguards at the end of the lake whistled her out of the water.

But during the times when the scoreboard read zero, I must say, I maintained my composure and held a positive spirit. I knew every snag could have been a huge bite and every stick a state record. When the times weren't as exciting as I would have liked them to be, I always seemed to amuse myself.

" Hey dad."

" What."

" I got another seaweed fish."

" Hey dad."

" What now."

" Got a lily fish."

" Hey dad."

No response.

" Yep! It's definitely a log fish."

" Hey dad."

" Josie what!"

" A piece of plastic fish. That's pretty rare huh."

But man there were some fish that were so big, no one would believe me! Not even my dad, and he was usually right there. My rod would be bent tip to tip and would be bouncing around to and fro, ready to snap.

" Dad, look at the size of this one. Holy comoly look at this thing. It's… It's…"

" The bottom."

" No way! Its Old Walter. I know he's in here somewhere."

I found out later that sometimes they were logs. They had a tendency to float up after my line would snap. But there were a lot of times I knew it was a fish. Perhaps not your everyday fish, but hey, I wasn't your everyday fisherman either. " Dad, could you imagine?"

Stark Cries

They were special times for me… It always seemed so peaceful there by the water's edge. But I knew when we went home things would be different. I remember how well my stomach would drop as we pulled up to our house on Terrace St.

"Get out if you don't like it. Get the hell out of here."

"Mom don't…"

It sounded like gunshot.

"No, oh no." "Why? I didn't do anything! I didn't do anything!" Dad's belt was thick and hard. It would leave welts on us for days, sometimes weeks.

It happened in slow motion this time. Maybe I was supposed to see it all. Maybe I wasn't supposed to miss one single bit. Reane and Venesa ran towards the wall. Venesa huddled in the corner and Reane stood over her. Dad was enraged. His demon eyes peered over at me briefly. "No! " Reane pleaded.

I turned my head away and pretended not to see. In the faint corner of my eye, I watched my dad's arm cock back. The belt fell and his fingers squeezed tightly shut. I closed my eyes, but forgot not to listen. The sounding of flesh striking flesh cannoned in the musty off-white living room. I looked up only to see a streak of red, zigzag in the air. Back and forth against my sister's beautiful face it followed. My mother grinned in the background. The stark cries continued upstairs. Sarah needed her fair share.

It went on for no less than an hour: the screams, the punches, the wonderful disaster of life. And it was just another day. Ten or more dishes lay broken on the kitchen floor. Close by, the garbage can lay knocked over. Coffee grinds covered over the labels on two or more beer cans, and that stupid mutt dog thought only to get a quick fix. In the midst of all that was happening, his clever ignorance was the only thing keeping me from believing this wasn't another nightmare.

I saw it all. I watched it all and could do nothing to stop it. The phone was off the hook beeping in the background. I tried to focus on it so I didn't hear the anger.

I looked at it all one last time. I had given up hope it would ever change. And so I ran. As fast as I could, I ran. I heard God's name and mine in the distance: "Jesus Christ. Josiah." But I didn't stop. I just kept on running. All the neighbors were home. Their doors and windows were wide open. No one had come to help or had even called the police. We lived in a good neighborhood; These things didn't really happen.

" Josiah come back here. Josiah!" It was Reane's voice. She was my older sister. She was a mother to me. "Josiah stop. Little kid…" That was me, the little kid.

She walked me up the road and in her embracing way spoke with me. We didn't look around much when we got in the door. Dad was cracking open another beer in front of the Giant's game. Mom was doing something in the yard. To them it never happened. And so I lay in my bed, waiting for night to fall and cover the ugly colors exposed by light. Ten minutes hadn't passed when I heard mom coming up the stairs. I could tell by the way the steps creaked under her feet it was she. My door opened. I nestled closer to the wall and squeezed my stuffed polar bear in my arms.

" Josiah."

I would not respond.

Mom got into the bed and put her body close to me. I felt scared and out of place.

" Do you still love mommy?"

I gave her the answer she wanted to hear. But it was a lie. I waited.

" Does it bother you when me and your Dad fight?" I felt her warm breath on my cheek.

She enjoyed when I winced there in my fright. For she was my devil and this was my hell. And from there I closed my eyes so I would not cry. This was her solace but not mine. Her hands found their way under the covers and from there, nothing. Death. Then, sworn to secrecy,

5

taking a vow of silence that would not end until my will was broken, I hid myself behind the dark violet shades.

We took things day by day. That was the only way to survive. We dodged the blows the best we could, and rebelled whenever freedom unleashed us into the world.

Country Kids

Thank God things were better away from home. We were good old country kids, just an hour from the Big Apple. Charley was my best friend. I met Charley in second grade when I switched schools.

He and I both had Mrs. Adams for a teacher that year. She had big brown eyes like a horse and she smiled like one too. I remember there were these two girls in our class, Sarah and Lisa. They were wild women. When Mrs. Adams would go next door, they would run up to the chalkboard and flash the class. This was a sight to see.

Charley lived down on Strawberry Lane. I would hang out with him every day. His house was different from mine. He and his two brothers, Guy and Derrick, all had motorcycles. His mom, Mrs. D, was the best. She had a big butt and was chunky, but she had the kindest heart in the world. Mr. D was really great too. He had a thick mustache and a little potbelly that hung over his belt. Sometimes his shirt would ride up so you could see his belly button.

The Dutchess' lived by the woods in a quiet neighborhood. The woman whom the street was named after was still alive then. I thought that was cool. She was as old as the street, and she lived on it too. When I took the trails to Charley' s house, I would always pass by her house.

Charley and I were tough country kids. We both loved the woods and would spend hours exploring them. One of the places we liked to go was Lark's pond. It was only a five-minute walk from Charley's. Lark's pond was an old man-made pond that was used to make ice for people's iceboxes when Charley's dad grew up. It was stagnant and its whole northern end was filled with cattails. Even though it was small and shallow, it was filled with large carp.

The carp were hard to catch. We heard that people would just put on huge trouble hooks and snag them, but Lark's pond had too many sticks and weeds to take that approach.

A Fish Tale

Weeks had gone by. Charley and I were tired of our efforts. We couldn't even get the bread to stay on our hooks, let alone catch anything. No matter what we used whether it was soft-moist bread, or hard bread it just wasn't working. One day, when we were getting B B's from Guy's room, I noticed a strong bow with a spool of string attached to the front of it. Close by, in the corner of the room, an arrow with reversed spikes leaned against the wall.

" Charley, what is that?"

" That there's my grandfather's bow-fishin gear. He gave it to Guy you know."

" Man, that stuff would work great for the Carp!"

So Charley and I embarked on our fishing expedition, filled with eagerness. We journeyed through the back woods, crossed over Mt. Sunrise Ave., and went directly to our favorite spot.

" Charley lets go over by the cattails. I see their backs out of the water. We can get some clean shots." Our strategy was flawless. We would capitalize on their vulnerability and reap a long awaited reward.

We made our way along the steep embankment. Above us, the busy avenue. Near Pat's Deli someone laid on their horn. Charley and I turned to make sure they weren't beeping at us. " Holy shit, that scared the shit our of me." "No shit, " Charley laughed.

"Alright this is good here." My feet sunk in the soft pond bottom as I walked. " Alright, are you ready?" " As ready as I'll ever be." Like two cats prowling on their inferior prey, we crotched low to the murky water ready to pounce.

" Ssh hush up." I unraveled about twenty feet of line, and drew the bowstring back to my cheek. Aiming at a large fin, I released the arrow. Swap! The nearby carp broke water and swam away. Charley and I ran up to the shore and pulled in the line. The arrow seemed to be embedded in a log of some sort. The two of us pulled. All of a sudden, an enormous carp started flipping around in a mad panick. We had hooked him! Charley put his hands out in front of his face. I continued to tug.

It wasn't but five feet from shore, when the spikes slipped back through the fish. It was loose! "Get it Char! Get it!" The water splashed all around us like we had harpooned a man-eating whale.

In the midst of all the commotion, Charley got hit with a chunk of mud, right under his nose. " Smelly horse shit!" I ran and giggled.

Charley's face turned bright red. " Come hea ya dumb fish!" His chest hit the shore, and his arms plunged in. But the ground was slick, and so he slid face first into the pond and nearly kissed the tale-end of that fish.

" Oh my God! " I cried. " No fuckin way dude!" Charley squirmed to escape. His hands disappeared into the mud and his face smacked the water. And off it swam.

Charley managed to get onto his feet. " I can't believe it!" I roared rolling on my back. With a muddy smile and only one shoe, he sloshed his way back to shore. I moaned with rib pains. But just when I started to recover, Charley slipped and his feet flew up in the air. He landed square on his back. After lying there quiet for a second or so, he let out one cough. We both found that cough so funny.

" What dah hell!" he yelled. " No stop! Please!" I pleaded. We rolled on our backs together... " Char, I think I peed my pants."

That was one of the many famous fishing stories Char and I had.

Whenever we trudged up to Charley's house covered with mud, Mrs. D would yell from the kitchen, " Down to the basements boys." So we would stick our stuff in the wash and then pig out up stairs. His mom always had a tun of food in the house-- that one cabinet. The craziest thing was he didn't have to ask permission to eat it.

Down the street from Charley's was the stream. That's what we called it ' the stream.' " Hey Char do you what to go down to 'the stream?'" We would play in it during the hot summer months when we weren't at Mt. Sunrise pond, our favorite spot ever.

The stream ran down from the woods, then ran through someone's property, then it went under the street and a little farther down it ran through a really long, dark tunnel and came out somewhere else. We would go cray fishing there or some times just sit in it and cool off. Sometimes, we would climb in the small tunnel, or slide down on our butts. I would make Charley go first to clear all the cobwebs. He would come out the other side with cobwebs all over his hair and shoulders. He would also have these little eggs all over him. Sometimes he would have the spiders. It was so funny when he did. All I had to say was, " Spider!" And he would start squirming and brushing himself off. Eventually, he caught onto my schemes so we had to start taking turns going first.

When we wanted to fish for bass at Mt. Sunrise, we would go down to the stream, and catch minnows. Along with the cool stuff at Charley's, he had this minnow net that his grandfather had given him. It had sticks on both sides and lead sinkers to keep the minnows from swimming under. Char would go up stream about ten feet and then he would walk down stirring up the water and rocks. When he got close, I would pull the net up and we would examine the catch. " Lets get the crays out of here first." Charley would always say. " Char what are those." " Those there are nymphs." " Oh." We never kept them or the pregnant mom minnows. Charley made us put them back. We took turns picking up the others one by one as they would squirm around in our hands. Sometimes, I would just get grossed out and would throw the things up in the air. Those we called flying fish. Charley would let those ones go too.

Mrs. Dutchess would drive us up to Mt. Sunrise, since it was too far away to ride with tackle. We would always hear them testing bombs at the arsenal. If the explosions weren't going off there, they would be going off over at the quarry.

Mt. Sunrise was a spring fed, man-made pond, once used as a coal mine. The Bashe House, an old Swiss mansion used during the revolutionary war to built ammunition was close by. Mr. D said George Washington spent nights there. We would ask him if he ever met George. " Ha ha, but one day you'll be old like me too!" He would rub his pooch belly like there was a baby inside. Charley said it was his baby.

Back Woods

It was a hot August day when we set out hiking from the western banks towards the Bashe house. Charley's father told us the basement of the house was used as a dungeon. Fascinating.

Occasionally, we would pass an old foundation of a home, striking an unsettling chord within us. Here in the haunted timbers pieces of the past remained. Canon balls and musket shot, arrowheads that were even older. We would dig for them, but never would we hold onto what we found. It wasn't right to steal from this land.

Whenever we spent a lot of time in those woods, it got strange... The woods would speak to us when all was still. We listened.

The Bache House sat catty corner to Mt. Sunrise Rd and the driveway of the rock quarry. We could see through the hot waves coming off of the road, huge dump trucks lined behind the gates. Behind them the mountainside hunched.

The trail abruptly ended where the forest had been divided by the road. Across from us perched the Bashe House. It cleared the trees and threatened the horizon; It confounded our feeble minds.

"Charley, lets go 'round back so no cars see us." We were scared.

The seller doors were like ramps. I walked, intentionally keeping off the rotting wood. Charley boosted me from behind.

" Wut do ya see?"

" Not much... Looks like a livin room. There's a fireplace."

" My pop said there's one in every room."

" I see an old newspapa."

" Wut it say?"

" May... fourth. Seventy nine. The rest is dark."

Charley lowered me down and we both walked around to the back porch. " Somebody sure don't want us in hea." Two birds fluttered out of a whole underneath the roof. Charley and I quickly looked up. " Shit."

The doors were bolted shut and the solid glass windows could not be opened. " I found it. We can climb up the chimney there, and then walk up that part of the roof and get into the window."

" That looks hard to climb. Wut you gonna do, break away du winda?"

" Yeah."

" I ain't walkin on dat top floor. Your libel to fall through. ."

" You're right it's dangerous."

Tempted.

" This hea's the only way we gonna get in." Charley pointed to a small window in the foundation.

" We gotta have gear."

" Well, maybe we should wait for another day. Let's get movin, the trucks are comin."

We walked along a dirt road, through a meadow and to an old church. Was this the one we heard so much about?

The shade receded and the hot afternoon sun made us wish we were swimming again. Tall bunches of grass grew out of what appeared to be a parking lot. We tiptoed along the front steps, ready to run at any given moment.

" Charley walk slow." I whispered, " There might be homeless people livin in there." Charley led the way in. Red paint was sprayed across the alter. Symbols. What exactly, I couldn't see. I waited patiently as my eyes adjusted.

Bottles of alcohol scattered about, used condoms and blankets. Charley and I stood still in our tracks. A satanic cult used to meet in an old church, in the Mt. Sunrise region. I didn't even have to ask Charley if he was thinking what I was.

A rat scurried into the corner. A stair case. We walked towards it. " Be careful, there might be bums livin down there." I whispered. " Josiah, you hea dat?" " No wut?" Sounds like a car." " No one comes back here."

I started to go down stairs. Charley followed cautiously behind. A car door slammed. " Shit, I heard that!" We both ran towards the door, working our way through its broken frame. I reached back to help Charley.

" Char, move your fat ass." " Josie!" " Wut?" Charley's eyes strained upwards. " Is dat a hornet on my head?" (Charley was deadly allergic to bees.) " Shit! Wut I do?" " Shoo it away." I swapped his head as hard as I could. " Fuck!"

We ran for the road, but stopped dead in our tracks. " Oh shit!" Charley said. " Oh shit!" Two policemen stood less than twenty yards away. We made a hundred and eighty degree turn and began running again.

My vision bounced on all sides. I turned around to see. In the distance, they galloped. One was tall and the other was stout. The shorter one was definitely the more comical of the two. He insistently held onto his belt to keep his pants from falling.

Charley, to my surprise, had stopped a little ways back. Hunched over now, his head lifted with a smile. It was then I realized he was showing the public authorities, his private treasure. A heroic endeavor.

" Wha whoo!" I yelled with laughter. Charley started slapping his bare ass.

The miles soon passed, though the woods went on forever. I turned around one last time only to see that empty church. Charley looked at me and then looked away. I had been there before: Gazing back. Wondering what it was. The dirty, white walls and broken windows. The emptiness inside. I was young, too young to understand.

I trusted Charley to get us out of there that day, and he did. Little was said for I was scared, though hardly let on. Exactly why, I did not know. Nevertheless, I was uncomfortable.

Charley and I didn't talk about that day again. Nor did we ever walk down those trails together or alone. We had felt things that we couldn't quite explain and so we tried our best to forget.

The Picture on the Wall

Sixth grade. I sat at our dining room table, slurping from a small, wood bowl. Mom was out late.

I believed that I was fortunate. That the Lord had been good somehow. I worried a lot though. I worried about the things I couldn't quite explain. The things that I knew were wrong, but that happened anyway. There was a fear growing inside. A fear of what the future might hold. It was 1988.

My sisters were all out of the house now. There was no one there to talk to. Sarah was in and out of jails and mental institutions. I didn't get to see her anymore.

Mom and Reane no longer spoke. They hated each other; I couldn't understand why. And Venesa too was gone. I could remember when she left for school. The picture on the wall was taken the day she left. Faded colors in a frame. Hers was the picture off to the side.

After she went away, I was filled with sorrow. She was a friend and now she was gone. When Cheers would come on, I would cry. We used to watch that show together you see, and almost every night we would sing the song together. Nesa would take the remote and pretend it was a microphone, passing it back and forth as we exchanged lines. Sometimes she would shake her hair like a rock star. That would always make us laugh.

I missed her. Occasionally, we would talk on the phone. She said art school was really hard. She said people were really weird there and had different color hair. I guess we both felt alone in ways.

I missed everyone, even Dad sometimes-- him and mom separated. I made sure to pray to Jesus every night for them all. He was my imaginary friend, and I thought he would listen.

CHAPTER 2

One in the Barrel

It was a Tuesday morning, sometime in that early November. I can still remember what I was thinking before life's circumstances made an offer I couldn't refuse. " If I could end it I would. If I would only dare..."

Tyler Labrock was preoccupied with the happenings from the day before and couldn't help but share his news with great enthusiasm.

" You're never gunna guess wut happened to me yestaday?" We looked at him doubtfully.

" I found a gun."

"Tyler, you're full of shit!"

" Swear to God man. It's by my house in an abandoned shack."

" Talkin smack again, huh Tyler. Last week ya outran a pit bull, this week ya found a gun. You're full of it!"

" Swear to God man. There's a bag of knives and machetes in there too."

There was something about the way he was saying it all; Scottie and Oogus noticed it as well. I could tell by the expression on their faces. There, was something more to this one. It could very well have been true.

Without further thought Scottie looked at Tyler square in the eyes, "We're comin over afta school." He took the words right out of my mouth. If there was an adventure to be had, I was in. Scottie and Oogus agreed.

When school finally let out, we wasted no time. Each of us went straight back to our homes and grabbed our bikes. Within minutes, we were off to Tyler's. Tyler lived all the way on the other side of town. He actually lived in Arlington, which was full of Hispanic immigrants, but the majority of his property was in Salsborough so he went to school with us.

It was a gray, cloudy day. A breeze blew through the barren trees. Wet leaves covered the sides of the road. We rode with caution out of the village, and down past Norway Park, where just before, we passed the power lines. There was a sign that would always catch my attention whenever I rode by. 'Danger Do Not Enter.'

We pedaled to speed, and the air was cold on our faces. Little was said. An anxious wait. The short cut by Carme's creek was dry and well defined by this time of year. The bogs had ebbed to the boundaries of winter months. It was a quick and almost effortless pass.

By the time we had arrived in Arlington it was four o'clock.

"Wut du hell took you guys so long?"

" We got here as fast as we could."

" I've been waiting foreva. Leave thu bikes in back. We walk from hea."

It was an ominous venture to the location. Tyler must have glanced over his shoulders twenty times. We passed police lines drawn across an area of swamp.

" Tyler." Scottie questioned, " Wut are them for?"

" Shh, keep yu voices down. Don't make a lotta noise."

" Tyler wuts wit them police lines?" Scottie whispered.

" They found a dead man layin in the cattails. See their all smashed up."

" No shit? When?"

" Three days ago."

" Can we go back now?" Oogus griped.

" Wuts a matter, Oogie scared?"

Tyler chuckled, " Nice town ain't it?"

The building was on the other side of the cattails. It looked more like a house then a shack... a pool hut of some kind. (Tyler insisted no one lived there, but I couldn't help but doubt his facts, his intentions.)

We crouched down under a covering of small pines and examined the area. The building was small... Overgrown by thickets and shrubs; It was hard to see much at all.

" Tyler."

" Yo."

" Is that a window?"

" Yeah, it's a winda. You can see it from there." He pointed.

" Josiah. Oogus and I will wait here. Go and check it out wit Tyler," Scottie injected.

" All right Tyler. You cool?"

" Yeah, lets go."

Tyler hunkered low to the ground, running directly up to the window. I followed behind. The building was dark inside. All I could see was the reflection of the tree in back of me, the highlights of my pupils. Our breath periodically clouded the glass.

" Jos, right there man. Yu see it?"

" No. I can barely make out a thing."

" Yo right there."

" In the case?"

" Yea."

I needed no further confirmation.

" I'm goin in."

I looked to see if anyone was around as I ran to the far side of the building. I opened the heavy door. Dark inside, a dim light came from the window. I ran over, looking up at Tyler. His eyes were wide, straining to see me. His mouth held open. I watched as his lips formed the words, "Oh Shit." He was frantically pointing over to where the gun was. I reached down and fumbled around, trying to feel for it. My foot kicked the case, and I heard it slide across the floor. I chased after it.

My heart pounding... Temples pulsating as I scrambled. At last! I grabbed it and ran for the door, but the gun thunked behind me. The empty case... I looked up at Tyler, laughing outside, " Oh shit. Oh shit!" I reached back, fingers curling around the cold revolver and then ran again: Kicking a hubcap across the floor, and collapsing a table next to me. And as I reached for the door handle, it swung open from the other side. A figure came running towards me. My heart fell within my chest, and the hair on the back of my neck stood on end. Our bodies collided, and I fell to the ground.

"Oh shit. Sorry dude," the shadow spoke and jumped back up. It was Tyler- running to gain the plunder. Outside. The door shut behind me, and I ran like hell.

From a hundred yards away a truck drove down the gravel road. Scottie and Oogus came to their wits, running for the woods; The woods were our escape.

Like a pack of wild animals, we sprinted along the trails. Bushes whacked our faces. The briers cut our sleeves and arms. Behind me, I heard their howls.

I ran. The Colt revolver bounced and wobbled in my baggy briefs. I could hear the creek ahead, running down from the old bog pond. I jumped with all my might, but caught foot on a root. I fell face first, landing in the cold stream, on the hard stony path. The pistol flew from my jeans.

I could hear footsteps thudding louder from behind... I rolled off the trail and put my hands over my head. No one came. I waited. Still no one came. Suddenly, the limbs dispersed. Tyler came leaping... " Oh shit!" we both yelled. Scottie and Oogus halted.

The four of us panted, half laughing. Tyler was holding an old bayonet in one hand and a clip to the gun in the other. He had a scratch across his face from the prickers.

My leg was freezing. My shoes were covered with mud. The Colt revolver lay low. Its pearl handle... Barrel silver and bold.

Quiet.

We gathered back ten feet from an old oak tree. Tyler ducked beside me. Scottie and Oogus held their ears behind the gray of their breath.

I held the pistol out in front of me. No cares.

Alone

I couldn't sleep; I kept reliving that day. Seeing Tyler Labrock's smile, the yellow ranch house, the old bog pond. I looked up at my wall. There was a picture of a soldier dressed in black, holding the same pistol. I took it out of the box, pulled the barrel back and pointed it around my room. Then crawled back in bed.

I stayed up for hours that night waiting, holding my eyes shut. It was darker than usual. It was only her and I left in that house. I was life. And so it was all justified: her loneliness and her desire, her wrath.

The gun was warm on my chest, a strange comfort. Another minute passed and still nothing. The aged house creaked like it always would, but my door never opened and she never came.

I woke, anxious and tired. I wanted to tell someone, but my lips were sealed. I kept to myself that day, my anticipation undisturbed.

After school Scottie and I went up to my tree fort and hid the gun. We placed it in a cabinet where we kept our secrets.

" Scottie," I spit my tobacco, " I wanna go back and get more bullets for this thing."

Scottie took a drag of his cigar like an old gambler. " Cherry," he liked his lips. " We have to wait a while... Let the air clear."

But the next day at school something happened. The teachers brought both of the sixth grade classes together. I started to get worried. Shit if someone snitched on us, we're dead.

Principal McGaven looked at everyone of us; Her head kept moving back and forth as she spoke. " Ladies and gentlemen I'm sorry for the disruption, but I had a visit today from two detectives. They brought to my attention something of concern. Apparently, a house in Arlington was broken into, and a hand gun was stolen. The police suspect younger persons are involved. If anyone can tell us anything in relation to this it would be much appreciated."

I felt myself getting warm. If any of us breaks we're all going

down. The bell finally rang, and we emptied the school. The troops gathered around, away from the premises.

" No one says shit. You guys got that. No one squeals?"

" Yo, they can't prove it 'less they find it. That's not gunna happen right Josie," Tyler demanded.

" No! I'll take care of it."

I went strait home after school and climbed up to the fort. I grabbed the bayonet, resnapped the case and shoved it in my bag along with the pistol. I walked out. No one around. I climbed back down.

I quickly wrapped the stolen items in an old rag. Then, I placed them carefully into a metal container, burying them in my yard. I covered the area with old leaves and then left for my daily run.

Bud was waiting for me. He and I always ran together after school.

" Young. How much today?"

" Ah, think I'm 'bout four ova."

We had matches on Thursdays for our home town, and on Saturdays we wrestled for the town next to ours to get extra mat time. The only problem was, we had to make weight two or three times a week.

Bud and I ran up Hill Top Point.

" Bud, I think I got myself into some trouble."

" Did ya eat too much today?"

" No. It's a lot worse. Can ya keep a secret?"

" Dude, you can trust me. Wuts up?"

" I stole a colt revolver."

" You stole a gun!" Bud started cracking up. " Josie your nuts! Where did ya find a gun." " Arlington."

" Wut are ya gowin to do wit it?"

" I don't know." I was embarrassed... "Protection."

The rest of the run nothing more was said, some small talk about the match. When I got home, mom was waiting to talk to me. "

Josiah, sit down. I don't have time for this," her self pity. " Did you take that gun?" She seemed worried others were involved.

" Swear on my life that you didn't take it." (Helpless during times of crisis.)

" Swear on my grave! That if you did I will die tomorrow." If it was only that easy. She put her hands to her hips and waited. "I didn't take it." Her disposition eased.

It was another restless night. I was so scared I began to cry. The next day at school I felt weak in my knees, sick to my stomach. I needed to go home. The school let me out much to my surprise, and Mom just happened to be waiting for me. " What's wrong," her mono-toned voice, not an heir of real concern. " Um, I banged my head at recess-- headache."

As we walked around the corner, I noticed an unfamiliar car parked in front of the house. When I entered through the front door there where two men in suits sitting at the table.

" This is Detective Wagner and Scott. Josiah." They looked like my Mom's tax guy.

" Hi." I put my hand up.

" Josiah." They nodded simultaneously.

" Why don't you have a seat."

I began to wet my pants; I quickly sat at the table.

" Josiah, we know you know what's been happening. We feel like you have information that would be valuable to this case."

" We're gonna ask you a few questions." " Everything you tell us is gonna be confidential," the other man reminded.

" Are you willing to answer these questions?"

I shook my head. "Ok."

I watched as the larger man took a thin black comb from his back pocket, and eased his way through his balding head.

" Josiah?"

" Hmm?"

" Where were you on Tuesday?"

" I was with my friends Oogus and Scottie."

" Oo... Oogus? Is that really his name?"

" Yessum."

" Who in their right mind would name there kid Oogus?" he murmured under his breath.

The other policeman shook his head in dissatisfaction and then intervened with a sobering breath of coffee, " Josiah where were you."

" I was at the field?"

" Was Tyler Labrock with you as well?"

I thought to myself-- everyone knows Tyler is not allowed to our end of town. Everyone will say that Tyler wasn't there.

I looked down at my hands which I was trying to keep from shaking.

" It was just us. Tyler ain't allowed up hea."

" Josiah, has anyone in school talked to you about this gun."

" Yeah, there's talk 'round school 'bout it."

" I'm going to be honest with you. We have reason to believe that you and your class mates are involved."

Mom conned me, " Josiah, you sure you didn't take that gun thinking it was a toy?" I shook my head no.

" Well we will be in touch Mrs. Roselli. In the meantime, here is our number if you need us." Mom seemed relieved. I went upstairs and laid down on my bed. " Holy shit, this sucks!" The clock ticked away the precious seconds.

The phone rang. I heard my mother faintly. I could sense her anxiety. " Josiah get down here!" " You didn't take that gun?" I looked at her, wishing I could end it all. All the nights she had crawled out of Dad's bed into mine. All the times she watched me bathe. All the times... She made me. I was sick.

"Sit down!" I sat down. Wondering what was going on. About five minutes later someone knocked on the front door. Mom walked back upstairs; Mrs Lucas was behind her, Oogus's Mom. Furious, she glared at me.

" Josiah, you did what to my son?"

" Tell me! Tell me!" She gritted her teeth and pinched my ear-- she wanted to kill me. I couldn't breathe.

" You threatened my son. Where is it! Where the hell is it!"

" Josiah!" My mother scowled. " Where's the gun?" ...Condemned.

Cradle's Lake

I had reaped what I had sown. In an iron field rusted and tarnished with my own carelessness, I walked and wondered. My eyes twinkled like stars ready to bum out, ready to fade away. My reflection, now haggled and grim, waved on top of the water. I watched a swan float with a rested air. " Why is a creature of such beauty so feared by the others?" I questioned, but did not care to listen.

There was a small, old cemetery across the way. No older than most, but they all seemed ancient to me. I watched a train of cars slowly traveling along the gravel drive. Solemnly on course.

I thought to myself, as I walked passed a common fishing whole. The memories of my youth....

Infant child

Child swan

How I wish I were you now...

Guiltless to the naked eye

Tender hearted out of the womb

Careless in a fallen world.

I'm nestled in my fears and sorrows

Living in vain

Low, dark and troubled

And through these tears I see your smile

Child swan

Infant child

How I wish I were you.

" You got lucky," I heard my Mom say. Her silhouette within the door way. I slowly rose out of my sleep.

" Wut are ya talkin 'bout?"

" Your charges were dropped." She twitched a brow.

" Then wut 's gonna to happen to me?"

" That's for me to decide... Get up!"

In that tense car ride nothing was said. I looked out the window and watched the rain fall upon the green cloaked country. Ahead of us I saw a huge, brick building, a castle. A large sign read 'Gray Stone Mental Institution.' Just beyond it some patients sat on several picnic tables, an odd formality. A dismal cloud covered the sun. There was fear. My fate in some strange way?

It wasn't but five minutes later when we approached the jail. The building perched on a small hill, and grew more intimidating the closer we got. Barbed-wire fences surrounded the grounds. I tried to think optimistically, but I couldn't.

" We take him from here Mrs. Young." "It's Roselli." The guard looked sternly at me. "You're comin wit us fella. Get a move on." I walked first, reaching to open the green door. A buzz sounded above me. " Open up. Don't miss du buzz."

We walked through a series of rooms... " Wait hea," the guard pointed. He left the room for a minute and then came back in. " This is where we check yaw mouth and yaw ass..."

" My ass?" I'll never forget it. I snorted so loudly the guard spit a lick of coffee. I quickly put my head down, pretending to cough.

" You find this funny Mr. Roselli?"

"It's Young."

" Whateva! Listen son, ya don't wanna to piss me off. You hear? Don't ya?"

" Yessum."

We walked down the west wing of the prison. I tried not to look up at the faces peering through the cell windows. " Most of the boys are at lunch." The officer opened a vacant cell, and we walked in. " This is wut you get, a sink, a shitter, and a bed." A southern draw started to sway his speech. "Notice there ain't no hooks or loose objects 'round. You can't cut the sheets to hang yawself. The material won't tear and won't hold yaw weight if it did."

He pointed up to the ceiling with his baton. "Notice dem cameras up theya. We watch you all day and night. " His eye seemed to sparkle when he said it. Homo. He looked me up and down and then raised his eyes brows. " Um... Come on, du nigus are gettin outta lunch."

I walked down the hall towards the lobby where mom was, reached for the door. " If you mess up again, I'll be seein ya," he grumbled behind me. The door closed.

Mom and I drove home and the minutes passed. For some reason it seemed she knew why I had taken that colt revolver, and could not scare me enough. She never came into my room again to satisfy herself, but this did not keep her from having her way.

Reflections

The weeks went by and the autumn air settled with the colors of the rainbow. The leaves withered and floated delicately onto their canopy of old. Life withdrew into boundless grasps. Soon winter made it's way across the land. Envious of the sun, envious of all.

It all seems like moments now, but then it was long and difficult. I was torn away and torn apart. The war waged on in my soul. And so I ran furiously trying to kill that part of me that demanded justice-- the part of me that would not die. An eternal fire.

The sweat streamed down the side of my face. I pulled my hat even tighter to hold in the heat. Flashes of the past... I fled. I saw my father's face-- a murderer... My mother biting her hand as she looked at me.

Back then there was no salvation, but yet I believed in something more. And so when I saw that small, brick church at the edge of the woods I ran to its doors to rest in its warmth. Locked.

I panted down the prayer walk, kneeling as a lowly one would, before a statue of Jesus. His face was calm and serene; His hand was extended and welcoming. I heard my teacher's voice in my head, " Keep your head up Josie." I began to cry; My tears became cold like rain. There was a still shiver in my bones. "Why have you done this to me?" I asked. But I would not dare listen.

I saw an image of mom lighting a candle at church. Rosary beads entwined her bony hands. We had the same god.

Breath rising above. The sky was gray and the trees cried for mercy. A light snow fell from the November sky. Deer in the far woods made their way through thicket. " I wish I could leave hea foreva, " I said with my head towards the sky. God had no time for the obvious. Like always, I returned.

1989

I made weight with ease as I usually did. Stepping off the scale, satisfied, I declared to Charley, " Under by a half pound. Not bad?"

" No," Charley shook his head. " But Headmen Valley's scales are heavier then ours?"

" How's your weight?"

Charley took a deep breath.

" 'Bout two over." He grabbed his rubber suit and wiped the cold sweat from the inside.

" You got time Char. The bus don't leave 'till three."

" Josie."

" Wut's up?"

" Good to have you back."

21

So the months crept by like the dawn of time. The days were filled with teenage tendencies and passions. I grew stronger in spirit and in will; Determined to survive. The fire burned inside. I dreamed of the day when I would escape from the place called 'home.' High School was just a stone's throw away. Then it would all begin. The years that would shape me forever. Those times were almost my last...

$\mathcal{C}$HAPTER 3

<u>High School Years</u>

For some, freedom never came easy. For others it never came at all. As for myself, I had to earn it day in and day out.

The days radiated with the hot August sun. Summer's last faded. Washington High was built on top of a small knoll-- closer to the skies, yet still so far from heaven; A prison with many cells. But it kept us sane somehow, a controlled environment was something we were well accustomed to.

The orange sun reached from the west. From the east breezes swept down and through the valley. I tied my shoes tightly and began stretching. I recognized players from the differant towns we had played in previous years. One kid was named Miles White. He was tall and had a long neck. His hair was spiked to perfection. He was kicking the ball around with an Italian fellow named Nick. I laughed when I first saw Nick because of his unusual profile. He had the largest nose I had ever seen on a living man. I recollected a billboard we would pass on the way to New York City. It had a nose that stuck out about fifteen feet, about thirty feet high. And so I wondered, family business?

Well the practices were tough. Guys were throwing up, and guys were getting taken out from all sides. Day after day the senior captains herded us into the woods for miles. Little did we know, they had predestined different players for the 'bobcat.'

I had no idea what it was until: I heard a war cry from the front-line, " Bobcat!" Instantly, three seniors came running towards me. " Oh shit! I'm a deadman!" They tackled a guy in front of me to the ground. The freshmen stood in shock as the once proud and noble warrior, received the biggest wedgie of his life.

There was underwear ripage. I'm sure there was pain involved, but it was highly entertaining. The victim hobbled back in line with a foolish smile on his face. As if to declare, " It's cool. I'm cool. No big deal." Too bad his underwear was six feet up in a tree and another six inches up his crack.

After a couple weeks of countless wedgie attacks, the woods became tactlessly decorated. We would run by the scene of a crime and reminisce, making some kind of wise, ass remark to the victim. (Pardon.)

Day One

I walked hesitantly down the large hallway, looking at all the new faces… Guys with beards, girls with boobs. I walked through the Senior Y. That was where the cool kids hung out. As I looked in front of me, I noticed Miles towering over the rest of the freshmen.

"Yo Miles wait up."

"Hey sup wit chue?"

" Not too much. You?"

" Nottin new but a damn thing… Yo dares Nick."

I looked over just in time to see Nick run into someone because he was looking down at his school map. Miles started cracking up. " What an asshoe. Can you believe dis guy?"

" So wut ya doin afta Sataday's game?"

"I don't know, sup?" (I tried my best to say it like Miles.)

" Vinny's havin a keggar in da woods. Wanna come wit?"

" Cool."

Saturday's game went pretty well. Although we lost, we played our hearts out. Coach didn't think so. " Here he come." Miles grunted and I zippered up the beer in my bag. We put on angry faces, so coach would think we cared. Walking by he screamed, " I can't believe this!" " Fuckin bullshit!" He slammed the door behind him.

Miles started cracking up. " What an asshoe. He actually dinks we're gunna win? Look at our team. We got a bunch of pansies asses running 'round the field wit dare dicks hangin out of dare pants! How we gunna win? Shit." Miles was right. Our team sucked.

There was a moment of silence. " Josie wut up?" " Yo. I was thinkin 'bout that analogy… very visual." We couldn't stop laughing. Especially at Doug Delani. He was a big Italian guy with an over grown ego and an underdeveloped IQ. He never realized most of the players on the team sucked. To him we always played like shit.

He would fabricate these ridiculous reasons why we lost. This time it was because we were "horsin around on the bus." Last time it was because we were "kickin like pussies." We just had to laugh. Until he would come out of his office of course. Then we would start banging the lockers with hidden grins.

" Here come du shit bag." Miles slammed his locker and then winked… We were always on the verge of ruining our act with that poised laughter. So Miles and I bathed in deodorant and ran out of there. As soon as we got to the street we let it all out.

Miles was such a cool person. He used to always make me laugh. Especially, when he called people assholes. He said it with style.

Miles and I made our way around the baseball field and into the darkening woods.

" Miles, how are we gunna find this place, its gettin dark?" " Its ahight I know deese woods-- grew up 'round hea. Hey Josieman, check it out." He pointed to a piece of underwear elastic. We both started cracking up.

" Those Orion's ain't dey?"

" I don't know, find the rest of 'em. If they got skid marks on 'em, then there his."

" Oh my God. You see dose dings? Thought I was the only one. Dats some crazy shit."

" So... wuts goin on with you and Tara?" Miles put his bag down and rezipped it; He heaved it over his back.

" Much betta... Sup wit me and Tara? Shit. You nosie little shit?"

" Yeah. She said you guys have been hangin out alot."

" Yeah, we've been 'hangin out.'" His face turned red.

" Ahh shit. Wut's up dawg?"

" Took her up to dat place you showed me, by du green pond."

" Yeah, past the hidden pines."

" Yeah."

Tara was one of my closest girl friends at the time. She had dated my friend Bones, but he took her for a ride. So I was pulling strings behind the scene-- trying to set her up with Miles. I knew how she was: She wasn't easy, but for a freshman, she partied.

" I bet you made out wit her."

" Pss, damn strait I did."

" I bet you felt those boingers too!"

" Pss, you asshoe. She already told you. Shit."

Wayward

We made our way deeper and deeper into the woods. The night had declared its victory; Shadows danced. Then, the firelight neared. Voices wove through the timber, whispering. We made our way slowly, sensing the channels of our steps.

The cool air quickened my breath. The bare limbs chattered in their heights. These times were mine: Clothed in nakedness, suppressed within. The stars peaked through the canopy above. Catching the dimmed sparkle in my eyes, they wished me safe keeping, sweet dreams and goodnight.

" Yo wazzup!" Miles shouted through the crowds.

The smell of marijuana filled the air. Beer balls were left empty and scattered on their sides. The music played, played and played. Miles pulled the twelve pack of Bush out from his bag. It was lukewarm now. " Hey Josie, hea's to Doug Delani." Miles reached for the ceiling of the sky with his beer.

There was a character named Patel; He was close to me pinning a can bowl. Patel was one of the many Hindu's around town, but more famous then all the rest. Many a story had been told of him.

"Hey, Patel." He lifted his head.

" Young how are you doing!" His reply.

" Alright. Wut are you makin there?"

" A homemade bowl. Do you want to puff?"

" Eh, I'm nursin my 'foetee' thanks."

I studied the crowd.

" You don't the marijuana?"

" No. I'm fine."

He was strange; Stranger than he might sound. He was fucking weird all right!

The fire blazed over our heads. Miles was a crowd pleaser; He would go on for hours with his stories. I drifted in and out of them at times-- had a mild case of attention deficit disorder. In this case, called horniness!

There was a girl watching me from the other side of the fire. She started to make her way to where Miles and I were. Miles was already hooking up with this girl April. I tried to warn him. Periodically, I would lean over and whisper " You'll hate yourself in the mornin." But he didn't seem to care. He would just swat me away without turning his head or removing his lips.

This girl with soft eyes was Jasmen. (I know what your thinking –stud. I know, what can I say). She was standing by the fire alone. I watched her, as she somberly kicked the coals from a log. I walked over to the keg close by and filled my beer. She acknowledged my presence with a reserved smile.

" How are you doing?" She asked. " Chillin, 'bout yourself?: " Thinking." We sat down by a log and kicked back a ways. "So wut are ya thinkin about?" I asked.

" I was thinking about you."

" Me?" Shawing!

" Yeah. I've heard a lot about you."

" Really? Tell me more." (I was the modest type.)

" Well tell you the truth, heard you were a little conceited. But in your favor, I must say, you look like a nice guy... But then again, looks can be deceiving."

" Right..."

" So are you saying the rumors of true?" She asked.

" Lets just put it dis way, how 'bout you get to know me, and let yourself be du judge. Your name is Jasmen right? I'm Josiah." She moved closer to me and rested her elbow on my leg.

" I know who you are," she said with those eyes.

" Right."

So I pulled her closer to me, our eyes met and we began kissing. Unbelievable! It was just like they said it would be. My older friends that is. They coined the phrase... I tried to recall. Jasmen's hands were roaming in places only my hands had been. Oh yeah, she helped me remember. "Mad play." That was it. "Mad play." I heard them say it all the time.

" Can we go somewhere?" We grabbed our beers and I took her by the hand. We led each other away from the light. In the distance, the fire crackled and the sounds of young innocence waned. Miles embarked on his own journey of discovery. I ventured through mine.

Jasmen and I held each other. Slowly, we each other down. I ran my fingers through her hair, gently, kissing her with every desire for more. I touched her breast and she breathed softly in my ear. She kissed my neck.

" So, I'm not just another one am I?"

"Wut?"

" Is this just a one night thing? Am I just another one?"

" Uhm. Ah... No." I said it like a bad actor on a first audition for a low budget foreign film.

" Well good... Anyway, I watched you wrestle last year..."

Jasmen unbuttoned my shirt and ran her hands across my chest. My heart grew heavy. My hands shook as if I was stealing something that wasn't mine. A side of me wanted to stop-- to quell that which I feared. But I didn't understand why.

" Josiah what's wrong?"

" Nuttin." I shook my head.

" Sure?"

" ...Yeah."

I reached for my beer, guzzling it the way dad had so many times before... as if it could remedy the feelings I could not explain. I started to unbutton Jasmen's shirt. Her skin was soft and beautiful. Everything about her seemed so pure and fragile. Though I was guilty and dying.

An ominous presence hung over me. I was condemned and locked inside a perverted body. Somehow she knew I couldn't go any farther. I could tell by the way she looked at me in that darkness. We continued to hold each other, finding warmth in each others arms, but never before was I so well aware of that void within myself.

Prelude to Madness

Lights flashed through the tress; Voices ran-- two kids towards us, shattering the slumber of our touch. " Yo chill." The bodies got closer and closer. I knew that they didn't see us. " Yo wut's up?" I startled them, but they recognized my voice. Panic stricken and glazed they hunched over trying to catch their breath. " Josie Five-O! Cops here!" " Oh shit!" I saw the flashlights coming down the trail.

" Shit. Let's go!" I lifted Jasmen by the hand, and we started to run, dazed and scared out of our minds. We turned off the dirt road, trampling over everything in our path. Their lights were getting closer, dog's barking louder. The sticks beneath our feet breaking, cracking like whips. They were on to us!

Our eyes searched for a way out. Hands waved blindly before us as we scurried deeper into the ravine. Rigged trees... Darkness... Chaos.

Farther and farther we made my way off the trail. Suddenly, the ground beneath me gave way. I fell face first landing with a heavy thud on my hands and knees. I saw colors, then black. Footsteps faded... Then, the dogs behind.

I was stricken. Crawling in a stone foundation. My fingers grabbed at the rocks; I fell back in. My knees and hands, bleeding. Heart, racing. I trembled. Desperately, for anything...

" Josiah!" I tossed and turned. " Josiah! It's me wake up!" I felt a warm hand on my shoulder pulling me back. Light shined in my eyes.

" Wut are ya dreamin 'bout? Wut happened tonight?" Miles squatted by the bed. He was laughing. " Shit you are."

Dreaming? It didn't feel like a dream. I looked down at my muddy shoes and smelt the beer and campfire smoke. I reached down-- the cuts on my knees still tender. "It's a good ding we didn't get busted." He smiled. " Just keep it down Josie man, you're gunna wake my parents. Dam." The lights dimmed to blackness.

Fall Days

Monday rolled around way too soon. I had spoken to Miles on Sunday. From what he told me, Saturdays bust got pretty messy. It was about eight o'clock when he called. I was just coming in from my run.

" Josie wut up?"

" Not too much. I just walked in the door. Hold on for a sec." I stretched the phone chord up into the bathroom for privacy.

" All right I'm back."

" So Josieman, the shit's goin down."

" No. Wut do ya mean?"

" The police cuffed a bunch of du crew. Brought 'em back up to school... You taken a piss?"

" Yeah, how can ya tell?"

" You sound like a freakin race horse."

Funny.

" So Miles who got busted?"

" Dey got like twenty kids."

" Are you serious?"

" Pss. Shit yeah! Marched du mutha-fuckas up to school, den questioned um."

" Wut did they ask'em?"

" Who got the beer. Who else at the party. Anyone doin drugs."

" Shit we're screwed."

" Pss. Dey can't prove shit. I'm not scared of those asshoes. But Josieman, listen to dis. When dey questioned dat hebob Patel, as soon as they ask'em the first question, he drew up all over du principles office."

" No shit?"

" I heard he puked like ten times… Nick counted."

" You mean Nick got busted too."

" Yeah." We both started laughing.

" That sucks."

" Hell yeah! They would have got expelled, if du party was over like fitty feet. They woulda been on school's property then."

" Oh shit."

" Hold on for a second." Miles clicked over to his other line.

" Hey Josieman you still dare?"

" Yeah, I'm right here."

" I got another call, so I guess I'll see you in school tomorra."

" Who are you gettin off with me for? It's Tara isn't it?"

" Wut an asshoe. See ya tomorra."

The first five periods flew by. I hadn't been pulled down to the office, and I had a good hunch that I wasn't going either; I was a puppet for the school.

" Sloppy Joes. I hate sloppy Joes. Wut else is there?" Miles pointed to something else.

" Wut the hell is that? It's not alive still is it?"

" I don't know. Look at dat shit. Man!" Our heads were three inches away. As if the mystery could have been solved with a close up.

" Is it some kind of noodles disguised in stuff?" Miles started cracking up.

" Noodles disguised in stuff? Maybe its puke. Sure look like it."

" Oh yeah, it is puke… Nice."

By now we were holding up the line. The lunch ladies scowled. Stomachs growled. We looked at each other.

" No Josie, I dink it shit."

" Really? Miles, I'm almost positive its puke. It can't be shit. They wouldn't serve us shit here."

" Oh but puke's OK. Mutha fucka. Look at it, it's shit I 'm tellin you."

" No, there are health codes against serving kids shit."

" Pss. Shit."

Miles and I finally got to the end of the line. Blue beard the lunch lady walked up. " It's Fridays pizza, and you don't have to eat it if you don't want to." We put our heads down and crept away.

Blue beard was a haggard, cranky lunch lady. No more ornery then the rest, but unique! Our older siblings had warned us about her before school began. " Watch out for the blue beard!"

Her nickname hadn't changed and rightfully so. Her bottom lip swung from the weight of a purple-blue growth.

" My God dats so discustin!"

" Miles, go over there."

We walked over to a table where Kile Jones, Me Dong, Nick Delosa and Carl were sitting.

" Why food services? Out of all du jobs. Man."

"Miles look!"

" Jones you eatin dat shit! You're one fucked up dude."

The whole table started cracking up; They had already tried talking sense into him.

" Yeah I like pizza." Kile spoke in an insane manner. " It's good."

These were my friends in the brig. They were my hope and fun and if it wasn't for them, I don't know what I would have done. Kile was a character. I had heard countess stories of him and his family, but never believed they were real until we met. His black, curly hair was already receding. I just figured he had such a sick head, the hair couldn't grow in some places. I concluded the majority of his insanity derived from his cranium. Thus, the receding hairline.

Me was a character of his own. I mean his name was Me... M...E... Me. This guy couldn't even make an emergency breakthrough on the phone by his real name. The operator wouldn't allow it. She would say: " You need to be more specific." He was a short Vietnamese kid with a spike that stuck up two months past its trim date. He ate a lot of pumpkin bread and seemed to laugh uncontrollably at anything that contained a hint of humor.

Nick I have already described, although I think his nose has grown since the last time his name was mentioned. To the right of Jones was Carl. Basically, looked like Waldo. Miles would always say, " I found him." Poor Carl would always be at the end of his finger.

This motley crew I ate lunch with; I was the only one that hadn't grown up in Fox Hill. I mean there was a cultural difference between these kids and Salsborough kids. They would only eat grape jelly. We ate either, although strawberry was preferred. I always called them pretty boys, but it never seemed to offend them. They were of a slightly elevated status, and for some reason proud of it. The Salsborough kids were definitely less refined. We liked to smell our own farts for crying out loud! From time to time, even exchange whiffs.

"So Josiah, I heard you were like crawling around in Miles's bed." Kile spoke in his high, eerie voice. (Kind of like Butthead on crack.)

" Were you like having a flash back or something. Ha. You know, after a traumatizing experience bad dreams are common. (This was probably the most Kile had ever spoken at one time.)

" You think you pretty funny Jones?"

" Yeah, I do. Ha ha."

The guys around the table laughed.

Unspoken Longevity

My head had been down for a few minutes; I was reviewing for a history test I had the next period. I had noticed it had grown quiet around the table. Raising my head, I looked to see what was going on. Everyone was staring like they were anticipating their worst fear; They were all focused on the same thing... Kile was pulling a hair out of his mouth. Apparently, the three-day-old school pizza was laced with a hair. Kile unfortunately had discovered it.

His eyes were bugging out of his head in complete dismay. He ever so slowly pulled the hair from his mouth, as to not break it. His lips were puckered and his eyes were crossed. He had reached the three-inch mark, and the hair just kept on coming. There was silence; no one spoke but we were one. No one knew when it would end, but we watched eagerly as Kile outlived the worst fear of the avid school lunch buyer.

Faces around the table grew. Lips moved unconsciously. Cheeks and mouths maneuvered along side as Kile reached the ten-inch mark. I watched his Adam's apple moving up and down. I knew the hair was coming right up his throat, through the chewed up pizza, and out into plain view.

The seven eyewitnesses were speechless, and all anticipated the bittersweet end. I noticed Me in particular. He was focused on the middle of the hair on which dangled like a sock on a close line, a triangular piece of cheese. At fifteen inches the end floated down. In complete shock, Kile continued to hold it out in front of him. His bottom lip quivering... The piece of cheese spun back and forth in a semi-circle. We were lost for words, and lost in time.

Then unanimously, everyone cocked their heads back, and burst out laughing. "HOLY SHIT!" Miles screamed. Nick laughed so hard nothing came out. He just sat there wiping the drool from his mouth. Carl ran to the water fountain when a piece of cracker took to his windpipe. Me was crying of course. He looked like Kong Fu master having a seizure; Me's spiked hair waved up and down from his sporadic jerks.

After about ten minutes we all gathered ourselves together. Sitting back down at the table Miles nonchalantly said, " Man did you see du size of dat ding." The chocolate milk suddenly shot up my nose. We lost ourselves in laughter again.

Gabriel Zeldis

Friday

That night we sat around Nick's living room waiting for the girls to call.

" Holy fra holy. Did you a see du size of dat ding. That hair was a so big." Me always had a way with words.

" Shit, dat mutha fuckin hair was huge," Miles replied.

" You guys memba du time wit Mrs. Jones and du bleachas? We was all at dis football game and Mrs. Jones came to see little Kile play. Josieman, you've seen Mrs. Jones before right? Trust me, you'd know. She's like four feet tall and weighs about dree hundred pound. She has orange hair and little freckles like Kile ova dare. Shit, where is dat kid anyway-- supposed to be here ova an awa ago. Anyway, Mrs. Jones was walkin up du bleachers and just before she get up to du last one, she goes 'ut oh.' That fat ass rocked backwards and then Holy Shit! Dat lady fell like a wind bag from hell. She was knockin people ova like a big round bowlin ball."

" Oh... wut about Kile's a grandfatha? Do you guys a remember that?" Me seemed to entertain himself more than anyone else. Especially, if he'd been drinking.

" Grandfatha Drew. That's it. Drew Jones got hit wit a shrat metal in du throat when he was in the war. So he couldn't even a talk. They had to lock him up in the insane asylum because he went a crazy as he got old. They locked him up in his room all by himself and forgot to a feed him for like a two month. Dat poor guy starved to death; He couldn't a tell dem he was hungly." Me shook with laughter.

" You got sick humor bro?" (Nick always tried to make him feel as bad as we did after sitting through one of his stories. It never seemed to work.) Me wiped the tears from his eyes. " Zankyou Dildo Boy."

Nick had earned the nicknamed Dildo after some of the guys apparently found a dildo with purple veins in mother's room. We felt for the poor guy, but these things couldn't be ignored.

It was now around nine-thirty. The girls hadn't called and the guys were well out of tales. Just when I thought the fun was over, Boner came waltzing out of Nick's mom's room with lingerie on. The panther skin design that was outlived in the eighties would have been enough. But Mrs. D always took it a step farther-- the nipples were cut out. There stood the two hundred and fifteen pound football star in the lingerie outfit gone bad. Mat's face grew red with embarrassment. He jumped off his chair and pushed Boner with all his might back into the room.

Nick had told us a year earlier, that he had caught his Mom in the laundry room with some dude. He apparently thought it was the spin cycle. Now the once mythological rumors were becoming confirmed reality. There was obviously another side to Mrs. D.

At around eleven thirty, later after some of the guys had gone to Kile Jones' house, the phone rang.

" Herro dare." It was Me.

" What you guys doing?"

" We're still drinkin beers."

" Come 'round here, over at a Andy's."

I put my hand over the phone. " Yo do you guys want to go over to Jones'."

" Wut you dink?"

" Yeah I'll game."

" Ahight Josie tell 'em we comin."

" Me we'll be over soon."

The Capsizing

Miles, Nick and I were glad to get out of the house. The night was surprisingly warm. We made our way along the quiet back roads, which encompassed Loon Lake. Taking a small trail through the woods, we came to the top of the notorious 'trestle.' Or at least it was in my mind. There were about two- dozen Jones stories that had derived here. The Trestle was basically an old railroad bridge that divided two lakes. Loon lake now sat behind and Placid stretched before us. Our feet dangled above its waterfall, a warm mist fell cool on our faces, and silhouettes flew across the light of the moon.

The moon was full that night; It danced with a touch on the waves before us. Nick handed us each a beer. " Nothin better then a fine beer when the moments right." The moment was right and we knew it well. Placid was a beautiful lake. It was naturally spring fed and although it was private, my friends would sneak over to it all the time to fish. Kile, of course, was the most notorious for doing so. He had been busted so many times the guards knew him by name. But that didn't keep him from doing what he loved. " I keep my boat running over at Loon Lake ha ha, ha ha. So when the guard comes I just run over to it and take off." Those were the words of an extreme fisherman! An extremely strange one I might add.

" What kinds of fish are in here?" " All kinds, mostly Bass. If you go over to the northern end by the streams, there's some good trout fishin. Rainbows and Browns."

We stayed for a time, then walked along the tracks over to Kile's. A train sounded in the distance, and things were quiet again around the lake community.

Back then we were all in this thing together. The grass was greener. The skies a little more blue. Back then there was always friends around. Always a laugh to be had. Always an adventure waiting...

The clock struck twelve.

Footsteps patted on the hard pavement and soon Luke and Me appeared.

" You guys, you a neva goin to believe dis one. Kile's a wasted."

" Kile? Kile's drinken," Nick responded.

" Tonight he did. He took a freakin bottle of Jack Daniels and tried to guzzled the whole dam thing." Luke seemed rather concerned-- drama queen.

" Motha fucka?"

" We had to hide the thing from him. I can't believe it; He didn't take it away from his lips. He would have dranken the whole dam thing!"

We walked quickly up to the beach where Kile lay. Crazy and like an infant in the sand, he rolled around. I kicked the back of his leg. " Hey wut's the mattered wit you." Kile rolled over. He had drool down his chin and neck and there was sand stuck to it. I bent over to talk to him. " Looks like you got a little shake and bake goin on there." " Yeah so wut," he retorted.

Miles pulled him up to his feet.

"Kile look at chue. You all fucked up?"

"Yeah, ha ha. I'm fucked up."

"Ahight, good to see you fucked up den. You fucked up. I'm fucked up... Wut do you say we goin have some fun den?"

"I don't give a fuck," Jones whimpered.

" Ahight 'bout you give me du keys to you boat."

" Here they are. But be careful, it's No Wake Day. Ha Ha." Kile started cracking up. He went to lean over on a nearby tree, but missed by a mile, he toppled to the ground.

The crew and I walked over to the boats. (Some of us more sure footed than others.) Kile, Miles, Nick and I got into the motorboat. Me, Luke and Myron Cage, boarded the canoe. " You guys take one of us in there with you," they begged. But it was a done deal. We didn't want them in our boat.

They paddled the overloaded canoe out to the middle of the lake, while I tried to get Jones's boat started. " Choke the engine," the drunken CO-captain shouted with slanderous remarks. The old motor finally puttered up and smoke billowed.

Andy took a deep breath of thick air. " Ah the fresh smell of Loon Lake," he said with a twisted grin. Miles started laughing at him. " Jones ya really lost it."

" I lost it along time ago ha ha."

" Kile you know how to swim right?" I asked.

" Yeah. I'm a Loon Lake lifeguard... And one of the swim teams finest." Miles continued to laugh at him.

" Just makin sure. You know, just in case somethin happened."

"Josiah! Don't put the prop down too soon. Seaweed is the leading cause of engine damage!"

" Whateva ya say Kile."

By this time the canoe was well ahead of us. Its sides were sunken low, too close to the water. After we had past the 'hazardous area,' I began to floor the engine.

If I remember correctly, our canoe friends were mocking us because we had taken so long. Now, I don't know what it was that got into me. Maybe it was my beer muscles, or the fumes that had billowed out of Kile's boat. Most likely, it was my own sick and twisted mind. I spontaneously gunned the engine, and headed straight for the side of their canoe. Each one of them looked at me. " What the hell are you doing?" " NOOOOO!"

To this day I don't know how it happened; Every law of physics including the theory of relativity was defied. Somehow we flipped over. I came up out of the water last. Near my head, the ten-gallon gas tank floated. The waves smacked loudly against its sides.

Me and the guys in the boat were half laughing as they screamed to Kile. Kile was so drunk, he had no idea what was going on. His hands waved about frantically as he choked on the oily water. Lu jumped in. " Stand up Kile!" He yelled "Just stand up!"

Finally, Lu delivered the game winning blow-- a wet swap to Kile' head. Swack!!! Kile instantly stopped. Surprised to see he was in about five feet of water. Me was hysterically laughing and Nick was either pissed or just drunk off his ass. I couldn't tell. He gazed to the peripheral bounds with an expression that lacked interest of any good kind.

I swam back to shore and looked at the motorboat. It was half sunken, bow pointing to the stars-- the Titanic of Loon Lake. Me was still laughing and Miles was swearing his guts out. " My new mutha fuckin shoes!" he screamed. Andy made it back to the shore and staggered across the beach until he fell face first into a pile of sand.

By the time everyone had gathered themselves together, a cool wind had swooped down from the hills. Nick, Miles and I had decided to take the canoe across the lake instead of walking. Nick was in the front, I was in the back, and Miles sat in the middle.

Miles had taken off his clothes to dry; Goose bumps covered him as he shook from the cold. We were about half way across the lake when I accidentally splashed him with my paddle. He explained plainly, " If you do it again, I'll kick your ass. You pissin me off." Elaborating, " It's your fault we're in dis situation." Who me?

I shrugged my shoulders to his remark, nicking the water again with my paddle. He arched his back. " Ahh." Still looking towards the front he replied, " One more time asshoe." Nick turned around an angry man, " Would you guys chill out!" He swung back, and the overloaded canoe jolted.

We hadn't gone ten yards; I cocked my paddled back, and struck the water with all my might. "Ahh!" Miles screamed. He jumped to his feet, rocking the boat. Nick-- scared half to death. "What the hell are you doing?" Miles yelled so loud, two dogs started barking on the other side of the lake.

Like an old man without his cane Miles turned around in the unstable boat. He bent down and grabbed the side to steady himself. Then, with all the stature he could muster, he stood back up again. He looked down at me and grunted, "Let's go asshoe, right now. Come on. I'm dead serious bring it on." He towered over me. For an innocent bystander in my shoes, this would probably seem like a scary position to be in. There's only problem. All Miles was wearing, was his socks and shoes and his tidy whiteys. There he stood, like a proud Hanes representative who had just come back from a marathon. I didn't want to fight him. But seriously! His package sitting there looking at me like a big nosed monster. I couldn't hold it in any longer.

It was probably the most effective blow I could have ever delivered. Nick quietly snickered behind pointing up at the seaweed that was now dried to Miles leg. And so the minutes went by. Nick and I laughed harder and harder. Miles's color changed and his shoulders began to droop. His face looked like a little boy's would, watching his ice cream melt in the hot afternoon sun. Finally, he sat back down. " Shit," he said, and we floated away.

We docked the boat on the quiet shore. Three in the morning. Miles was looking out on the lake trying to see if his orange soccer shorts were floating around. Before that night had begun, I had pocketed a couple of Nick's pineapple bombs. He had told me that the bombs were waterproof, but I didn't see how the gunpowder was still good after capsizing.

Bent down by an old dumpster, I took my lighter out and tried the explosive. Holding the flame to the wick for about five seconds… All of a sudden, the sparks starting flying. Instantly, I jumped back and started running. Nick and Miles looked back to see what was going on. "What the hell." " Oh shit!"

We ran as fast as we could then… BOOM! The firework exploded, echoing across the lake. Dogs started barking. Soon, people's lights went on. We ran down the street as fast as we could. We had almost made it back to Nick's house when we passed his neighbors. They happened to be having a party on their front porch. To this day, I don't know what they were thinking, but their minds would be warped forever.

Sprinting; Miles led the precession. His long legs stretched out before him, as he cruised by in his tighty whiteys. Nick was a nose away, a close second. And for some strange reason, he was carrying the paddle. I was the last in the sequence- grinning from ear to ear, carrying Miles's shirt and hat. We looked liked three gay lovers who had been chased out of a romantic spell.

To make matters worse, I accidentally dropped Miles's shirt right in front of the party. When Miles had realized what had happened, he turned around. Like a blast from the past he darted right back into plain view, grabbed the shirt and started running away again. The crowd which had been speechless up until this point, started cheering him on. All we could hear was the distant roar. To say the least it was an odd night!

Into Exile

The last leaves had fallen, and the wind was cold. Winter skies buried the sun. The season was near to begin.

" We'll see you in spring," Nick said through his chuckles. Miles nodded. " Good luck dog." The guys headed for the showers, and I walked down to the room. Keith was already waiting for me.

" Good to see ya Keith." " Likewise Young." We snuck into the room around five. We were rusty, but the mats felt good beneath. Their smell, familiar-- musty and dry.

Six thirty came. I made my way over to the weight room. Anything to keep from going home. Anything at all.

Turmoil.

1991

" Coach."

" Hey son, have a seat."

" You spittin Young?"

" No."

Muller threw me his tin. Fine Mint, that's all he ever chewed. He packed the tobacco under his lip and pulled a newspaper from his desktop. He scooted closer.

" Well son, I've been playing 'round wit some things. I wanted to see wut ya thought."

" Hit me."

"Well, I was looking to see how we matched up to the rest of our county. The weight classes are stacked up."

"Young." Muller spit into his coffee mug. " Wut weight are you goin this year?"

" Twelves or nineteen."

" Listen son, I need your help. Suck down to three and we'll have a good season."

I put my head down; Sacrifice.

" I'll do my best."

" That's wut I want to hear. We need to bridge the gap in our lineup. Freshman and seniors is all we got."

" 1995 is the year."

The boys and I had talked about it before. There was a wave of talent that had swelled since the time we were young. Our county was fierce; We were at the tail-end. The years of sweat and tears would pay off when we were seniors. Until that day, we would pay.

Day of Season

Charley and I walked into the room a little early.

" Josie do ya remember that day on the beach... when you and I first wrestled."

" I'll never forget it. You kicked the shit out of me."

" That was the first time I actually made someone eat sand. Wut grade was that in?"

" Third."

" Dat's right. You came out for du team four months lata."

" I'll never forget the headlock you hit on me. Fuckin thing was sweet."

" You're tellin me."

Charley and I drilled around as the others poured through the door. Connelly. He was the first one I saw; The one I would have to beat to wrestle varsity. The others I was familiar with: there was Barrington, Tremmel, Carino and Samuel Faset. (Also known as Fat Set. He was our189 pounder.) There was Risen and Randy and Delcon the heavy weight. Then of course, all of us: Naville, Bonnam (known as Bones or Boner), Vachelli, Charley Dutchess and I. The rest of the guys were extras. They came and went, but weren't really there.

"Let's go men," coach yelled from the hall. We funneled out of the door. It wasn't a game anymore, nor would it ever be. We took our beatings when they came and struggled on. There was little glory, nothing to be dwelt upon. We made our way into the next season with heads held high, as men. Fierce.

1992

Our whole starting lineup, with the exception of two juniors, consisted of sophomores. As a team we did well. As for myself, it was one of the best seasons of my life. I was sucked out, but was the strongest I ever was.

I won match after match, tournament after tournament. I went on a twelve man pinning streak and put four others in the hospital. I made headlines and set the records straight. I pummeled the kings.

Over and over I trained through one of harshest winters imaginable. I ran in the snow, sleet and rain. I would begin my day early, drilling moves before school began. I would run at lunch and lift during physical ed. I stayed after practice to roll with the coaches, and I skipped rope for hours before bed. I would train for six hours some days and always felt like more.

During matches, while everyone else was on the mat line, I made it a point to condition myself none stop. And when I wasn't training, I would study other wrestlers. I wanted it so badly then. It tasted like blood.

Determined to be free, I had caught the heels of a fleeting hope. But something happened in those next few months that changed my life forever. My father was diagnosed with cancer. It was as though the crescendo of a large orchestra broke on a cymbal's crash. Silence; A silence I couldn't explain. I was scared.

Drifting... Storm clouds rolled towards the horizon.

$\mathcal{C}$HAPTER 4

Breaking

Dad would come over on Saturdays to see us. He was reading his newspaper like he normally did, drinking his coffee by the back door. Mom and I were moving chairs from the backyard into my trailer.

As I went up towards the gate, my eyes caught sight of dad. He was carrying a chair, barely. " Dad don't, it's ok we got 'em." Dad insisted on carrying it another ten feet. Then, with shaking arms he set it down and rested his weight against it. I tried not to care. Tried to tell myself this wasn't hard. But I couldn't. The tears welled up and put a lump in my throat-- couldn't swallow. I put my hand on his shoulder. " Wut are ya doin dad?" His reply: " I just want to spend time with you Josie."

We stood in the yard a while longer. The tall willow tree swayed. His hair blew across his wrinkled forehead. When I saw that his strength had returned, I reached out and he handed me the chair. He stood in the yard. His eyes, falling.

As always the doctors had a plan. Mom informed us that dad would be going in for an operation in September. The following weeks went by, slowly. I made sure I went to dad's regularly to do chores. We would eat together on Saturdays and would watch TV for hours. Finally, the time came.

It was about eight o'clock on a Friday night, when I finally got to visit him. I thought he would be ok. He wasn't. Instead, he was strapped down and squirming, in agony. His back was arching and his head was shaking back and forth: once to the right, then to the left. I saw his face as he turned. It didn't look like dad. He had tubes sticking out of his nose and mouth. Others were stuck in his arms. I wanted to run away and hide, but waited. Heavily drugged-- his eyes were sealed. I stood there. And in the halls no one stirred.

Just as I turned to run out, two of my sisters walked in, Sarah and Reane. Reane was a nurse-- I felt better when I saw her face. But Sarah, Sarah made the time slow. She looked at dad like he was a dead man-- a quivering look of despair. Her eyes were full of sorrow. Drowning. I could feel her hopelessness.

In the weeks following the operation, Dad healed. Soon he was well. He began eating again and gained his weight back. We would fish and eat dinner together on weekends. It was as if everything was ok.

The breath of life returned. I remember the day. Dad was sitting by the water, watching the ripples and sunlight glow. He was a hero to me. (He had not been a good man, but the child inside of me still looked up to him.) The skies were blue. The autumn wind like mercy. The waves crashed ashore.

Would I endure?

Turning Away

Mid October.

The rains had been coming down for days. Sounds of thunder, and I awoke. Four in the morning. From the window, I watched the lightening illuminate the rain. I listened. The whole last season flashed through my mind: the smiles, the tears and pain.

" Now on deck from Washington High, Josiah Young. And from Rutherford, Greg Murdock."

It was the last team tournament of the season, used as a qualifier for the regional tournament. The auditorium lights were off except for the spot light on the center mat. Wrestlers lined each side of the mat. Everything faded around me.

"Now at one hundred and twelve pounds from Rutherford..." He was staring at me. I was still, staring back. " James Murdock!" He ran out on the mat, waiting for me at the center. " From Washington High... Josiah Young!" My hood was pulled over my head. Our hands slapped together.

1993- Battle Cry!

Coach Muller walked into the room with a smile on his face. He was carrying a broken hockey stick with a torn, red rag on it. "Oh shit!" I heard someone say. " Red flag day boys!"

Our stomachs dropped as coach paced the room. " Two groups... ones drillin, the others runin." He put the clock on forty-five minutes, then turned the dial up on the thermostat.

Our group took off down the hall. I barreled in front...

We were about twelve minutes into practice when the first man fell. No one looked, we just kept running. After about fifty minutes we came around the corner, and the other group was outside getting a drink. " Get a drink and get yaw shoes on!" Coach shut the door behind.

We broke up into groups of fours and each group found a circle on the mat. Coach set the timer. " Aright hea we go!" He screamed. We slapped hands and coach blew the whistle.

Instantly, Naville and I locked up head to head. We tugged on each others necks. I faked a shot and Naville sprawled to the mat. We locked up again. Navi squeezed my head. He was pissed.

I ran him towards the wall. " Ahh, son of a bitch." He came running after me. So I reached up to lock up again, then dropped down and sunk deep into a double leg. I picked him up off the mat and dropped him down. Coach grinned from the side.

" Young, get yaw ass ova hea and see Woody!" Woody Norwood was our trainer. He had mended me countless times-- said I bled the worst out of them all.

" I might have to get this shit cauterized, huh Woody." I spit a gob into the garbage. " You might," he responded, "but for now this will do," and he shoved a cotton swab up my nose. " Ahh, soft plugs for a change." " Yeah, but dey don't come out so good." " Shit."

In the back of the room the heavy weights were banging heads; Bones ran Tyler into the rickety heating vent. Muller and Shapiro laughed. Shapiro was the assistant coach. A stocky man with cauliflower ears and a beard that would burn our faces. He beat the shit out of us.

The practice was soon over. Coach put the clock on eighteen minutes, and we lined up in formation. Conditioning was always last. " Start running!" We trudged along in place.. Our shirts were saturated with sweat; our faces were wet, bruised and burned. " Captains up in front!" We faced the guys.

Tired. Our eyes beginning to get sunken-in from weight loss. Skin, pale. The weight of the unknown future gravitated on our shoulders. It was another beginning... The trials-- victory or defeat. It was all but moments away.

Each guy had come from a different place, but we were all in search of something. There were heroes to be crowned and losers deemed. A perilous hope. Together into heartbreak. Together, unto the end.

Desperate eyes silently begged. There, they stared at me and I at coach and he back again. The empty glares. Broken shoulders and stain. Yet the battle inside answered.

" Hit it!" We all sprawled to the mat.

" Back on ya feet!"

" How bad do you want it!"

" Hit it!."

" Push ups!"

"Down!"

" Up!"

"Down!"

"Up!"

We called and they called back.

" Squat thrusts!"

" Sit ups!"

" Back on ya feet!"

41

" Come on now, yaw doggin it!" Coach pushed the clock back.

" Let's go Washington!"

" Hit it!" The guys fell to the floor.

" Hit it! Hit it! Hit it!"

" Get the fuck off the floor and sprint!"

" Single leg!"

" Jog!"

" Double leg!"

" Move yaw asses!" Muller screamed again.

" Let's go Washington!"

" Push ups!"

" Down!"

" Up!"

" Down!"

" Up!"

Captains yelled and responded.

" Monkey rolls!"

" Two minutes to go! Dig!"

" Let's go Washington!"

" Let it burn!"

We wrestled and rolled, sweat and bled like we were warring for our lives... Finally, the buzzer rang and the doors swung open.

" Alright boys bring it in... Good work today. Way to bring up the intensity in the room. Rememba, we have the Falcon Valley season opener in two weeks. We will start wrestle-offs next Wednesday. Coach Shapiro wut else did we need to say?" " Ring worm." " That's right. We have to make sure this season to wash and sweep the mats extra good. The league is crack down on ringworm. If yaw itchin, see me or Norwood. That's it." The guys headed out.

I changed my shirt, stretched out a little and started wrestling with Shapiro. Coach outweighed me by about forty pounds, but he wouldn't use his weight against me. We rolled for another half hour. By that time, exhausted.

" I'm out." I pushed coach away. " Keep ya sweat up." I walked over to the wall and crawled under the mat. " Young." " Yo." " Way to be." I nodded. " Josiah your gunna make it. Believe now."

I pulled the mats over my body, closed my eyes forever. Coach killed the lights. The door shut.

Sweat poured down my face. I lay, quietly underneath the dusty mat. Images of the past flashed through my head: Venesa on her knees praying to mother. "Stop torturing us!" Sarah's red face going through the sheet rock wall. Reane's misery of living another day-- stalked by demons. My Dad would sway at night. He hardly knew what hit him; He would strike too.

We were addicted to coming back for more; It was all we knew. I had become a ghost in the body of an old boy. A spirit in torment searching anywhere for somewhere. I was drowning in thin air, screeching at my knees, determined.

The coldness that ran through my bones... She was a murderer; She was the devil and she would always remain. The coldness left a chill in my bones that I could not escape. Even lying in that hundred and five degree room with a dusty mat pulled over my body and head-- there was her smile. The way she looked at me. Hatred-- I could not escape.

Voices in my brains. Distressed jury. I was pulled apart at my seams. That damn flicker-- light inside. I was petrified.

As the season rolled on, the haze and the pressures once more came to triumph. The stands of fans fueled me. There was the weight of a thousand tugging at my soul and a thousands more to come. I was back to my normal routine, making others pay for the things that no one knew of-- crimes kept in silence. I lived to bang heads and bleed out there on the mat, my desert home. The pain made me feel whole. The screams and moans, the aches and groans it was a savage fun I knew so well. My eyes shown fierce that season, for I was starving.

When my sweat had ended I gathered up my soaking wet clothes, and headed over to the locker room. Charley was the only one left; He was waiting for me.

" Charley ya still here?"

" Yeah, today's du study night. Did ju forget?"

" That's right... At least I don't have to go home right away."

" Let me bum a dip Char."

" Sure. I owe ya one there anyway." Charley tossed me his dip.

" Hawk's huh."

We sat in back of the locker room spitting into the floor drain.

" Josie wut's yu weight class look like?" Charley's eyes combed over the clippings.

" Pretty tough, I got Murdock, Binder and Hall again. Hall might bump up though, looks like twenty fives are easier."

" How 'bout yourself, how's your class look?"

" It's stacked. The counties there are gunna to be tough. But I could probably take du Districts.

" Here take this." I handed Charley the newspaper and headed over to the scale.

Coach made us sign our weights in and out daily. I took off my towel, breathed all my wind out and gently stepped on the scale. One twenty four and a half. ' How the hell am I going to lose the rest?' I thought.

Gabriel Zeldis

Season Opener

The Falcon Valley tournament arrived. We had sucked down for weeks- way too much, and way too quickly. Our bodies were in shock. Legs, weary from running in rubber suits and jumping rope in saunas. Our cheekbones were bulging out of our faces. Our skin, pale except for the bags that perched heavy under our eyes. I barely made weight.

I sat down by the lockers and waited for Charley. I knew he was going to be close. He had been jumping rope in the showers all morning and had left his sweat gear on the whole way to Falcon Valley. Charley had been over by a quarter pound for his first weigh-in, now, standing on his head waiting for the blood to fall.

" Dutchess you up!" Charley jumped down, took a deep breath out and stood naked on the scale, head tilting back. (As the blood fell back down the body it was virtually weightless.)

" All right, step off." Charley grinned over at me. " Man that's a trick." We grabbed our belongings and headed over to the cafeteria. The other guys had started eating.

This was now our ninth year wrestling together and third year wrestling varsity for Washington High. They were my family. I had laughed and cried, sweat and bled with them for years.

Anxiety welled within us. Coach walked in... A smile on his face. We didn't know if he had gotten laid the night before, or if we were in good standings; He had just come from the seating meeting.

" We got five first seats, three seconds and a third. That's excellent!" We passed around the charts, looking them over.

" Young you got second seat." " To who?" " Amstel Myers." " Is he tough?" Coach looked at me, " A brick-iron shit house." I felt my stomach drop, nothing I hadn't felt before.

Match after match we wrestled that day. Pummeling ruthlessly all who crossed our path. We didn't realize to what extent, until we lined up for the final introductions. It was an impressive start to one of the best seasons we would ever see. We were now juniors, and our long years of devotion were starting to pay off. My days of standing alone on the mat line were over. We had raised each other up from the bottom; Now powerhouses-- feared and respected throughout.

Coach brought us into the locker room, away from the crowds. " Lets pray." We gathered together on one knee. " Our father who art in Heaven hallow be thy name... " Our eyes fell. Hands, tightly grasped... Eyes met.

Coach slapped his hands together. "I want six minutes from each of you. Wrestle aggressively. Don't try any fancy bullshit!" He looked us in the eyes. " Work your moves. We're in a good place now. Don't fuck it up. Wrestle smart and stay aggressive... This is it! Bring it in." We all gathered around. " Let's go Washington let's take this!" " Come on guys this is it!"

44

With our hands together, minds and hearts as one, we raised our voices: shouting and clapping and slapping one another across the face, banging on lockers and heads, anything that would make noise. " How bad do you want it Washington?" "How bad do you want it?" "Raise it up!" Naville kept on screaming. I know heaven heard us.

The doors swung open. We walked. The gym around us, transformed. One mat now. Stands drawn to the center. The anxiety. From the scoreboard above our heads came a distinct hum; It sounded constantly under the murmur of the crowds. I clasped my headgear and pulled my hood over.

Two thousand eyes stared through the dark wilderness. The only light I could see-- amber hazards that lined the stairs; the dim radiance. Black silhouettes crossed our path. We waited.

The guys rustled around, and from the course surface of their nylon warm-ups came a consoling rhythm. The gods spoke and the main spot light turned on. The crowds unanimously stood to their feet as an intoxicating roar enchanted our fervent beings. Couch gave the front man a single nod, and we ran out.

I was the third weight class to go. The wrestler I faced off with had made it to the state finals two years in a row. Amstel Myers. He had placed first the year before, but I was fearless.

Twenty minutes had gone by. Bud came running off the mat. I couldn't tell if he had won or lost, for he immediately ran to the locker room. "Young you up." I ran across the mat to the head table. The head referee checked me over, and I ran back to my corner.

Muller got close. His eyes were like black stone. "You're wrestlin for six minutes. Work your shots. Let him up if you have to, but win on yaw feet!" I nodded my head. "How do you feel son?" I nodded.

Amstel Myers was waiting on the mat for me. He was running in place, shrugging his shoulders and rolling his head back. " Let him wait..." Coach and I stood still; He was the closest thing I had to a father, and I sacrificed myself to make him proud. Our stares were locked. Coach squeezed my hand, " Wrestle smart son... Alright do this!"

Coach slapped my back as I ran out on the mat. The crowds cheered. " Wrestlers shake hands." " Tables ready." The whistle blew. Myers shot right off the whistle; He sunk deep. I sprawled, but he kept coming after me. He drove me like a bull across the mat. I fell back tossing him over my shoulder. " Out."

The whistle blew. He shot and I sprawled, under-hooking his arms. I took my right arm out from underneath his chin, and forearmed the back of his head. His head hit the mat. I clubbed it again, and spun around. " Two."

I was on top now, my weakest position. Couch yelled from the sidelines, " Give em' one not two." I let him up. " One." We circled around and around. Frustrated, I ran after him and pushed out of bounds. " Lets wrestle on the mat boys." The whistle blew again. I shot a low single, standing to my feet with it. I squeezed his leg to my chest. Myers pressured my head.

45

Wheezing- arms weak, legs tired. " Yaw wastin yaw time Josiah! Get out the hell outta there!" Myers sprawled back and my grip started slipping. In a moment, I let go of his far leg and turned the corner. Driving my right shoulder into his quad, I spun around. The buzzer sounded.

We slowly stood to our feet. The score, two - one. An official took a coin from his back pocket. It whirled in slow motion. Fans watched eagerly.

"Your choice green." I looked over at coach. " Defer." I turned back. " I defer." Myers pointed down.

" Bottom wrestler set." "Ready?' "Top man." I knelt down on one knee, covering his hips with the other. I placed one hand on his elbow, the other one slowly across his stomach. The whistle blew.

Myers instantly stood up-- The crowds awoke. I threw him back down to the mat. A wave of silence. My hips were clamped to his, following his attempts to score. I watched the seconds of the clock. " Your stallin green!" The ref slapped the mat. Myers stood to his feet. Tied at two.

" You shoot Young! You shoot!" The parents and teammates yelled. Myers was tired. I knew I couldn't let him catch his wind. I pummeled my way in and worked for inside control. Ducking Myers head, I shot, and brought him fiercely to the mat.

His coaches yelled, " That's a slam ref," with a tedious call. " Let him up Young! Let him up and do it again!" Muller slapped his hands together. " One point red."

I pummeled in again, this time grabbing an under hook. Myers clammed his arms downwards and scooted his hips out. The buzzer sounded.

Fatigue-- unfathomable. The score was too close. I was a defensive wrestler, scoring mainly on my feet. Going into the third period with a narrow margin, was a common place for me to be. The pressure alone could make one crack. But I wouldn't. I never gave up.

" Green chooses bottom." Off the whistle I jumped to my feet. " One." The score, five - three. Working in I grabbed an under hook, jacked him up with my left arm and worked his head with my right. I snapped his head, picked an ankle, and threw my left arm up to the ceiling. " Two." I let him up again.

Myers was stunned. He took a poor shot trying to hang on a leg. I sprawled, whizzered him, and pressured his shoulders with my hips. Muller yelled at the top of his lungs, smacking his hands together with great force. Pointing down to the opponent he shouted, "Make him pay! Make him pay Young!"

I continued to pressure his shoulder. Then, with all my strength remaining, I shoved his head to the mat. I Grabbed his far arm, I chopped his support, and bumped his hip with sweet style. He rolled gracefully to his back. The crowd yelled in a queer fusion of discontentment and satisfaction, standing to their feet. " Deck him! Deck him!" My teammates yelled from my corner.

The ref's arm was suspended in midair. "...Three. Four. Five. You got three backs top man." I threw my arm across Myers's face. He moaned in discomfort. I ground my wrist bone across his face. The blood from his nose leaving a red streak across my arm. His shoulders wouldn't touch.

I knew I needed to turn him with a different hold. Remaining in good position, I created space with my hips, and allowed Myers to turn to his stomach. Quickly, I spun around to the other side, and sunk a half nelson.

" Run it! Run it!" " Stretch him out Josiah!" I draped him across my knee and ran to eleven o'clock. Again, I attempted to take his base away, but Myers reacted and stood to his feet. For a split second I looked up. My mother was in the stands. Then the fury came over me. I ground my teeth until they chipped and with the half still in, I stepped in front of him. Dropping my hips, I tossed him square to his back. Myers yelped. His coaches scream from the sidelines, " Come on ref! That's a slam!" " That's unnecessary roughness! Where's your head at?" But it was too late.

The ref jumped down to the mat. My back arched with a sleek curve, as my head angled to the ceiling. Myers let out a moan of underneath me. His shoulder was no more than a half an inch away. I arched back again, and while maintaining my poise, I continued to drive my knee directly into his face.

I could see the crowd cheering, but there was no sound. Coach was yelling, but I could only see his mouth move. It was all in a tidy, slow moment. Myers's coach dropped his clipboard and turned away. The clock ticked from nineteen seconds down. I watched as the ref reached a yard away, he lunged forwards. Then, I heard the crisp slap of his hand against the mat.

The whistle's blew around me; Then a wave of sound came to the center of the arena. The refs jumped in and pulled me off. I had blood across my body and sweat pouring down on my face. My teeth, pink. I looked out across the stands. She was gone, but it was not over. Never!

Coach clenched his fist, " That's the way Young!" I ascended to my feet. Myers coaches held their heads in disbelief; I had upset their top seat. Myers lay bleeding and badly bruised. I reached out, helping him to his feet. An imprint of sweat coated the mat behind him.

" Good match fellas. Shake hands." The crowd's cheer grew loud, as my arm was lifted high. " Coach Muller and Shapiro ran to me as I came back to the corner. "Way to set the pace son." " Way to set the pace."

The announcer began introducing the next weight class, as I walked towards the locker room. Faces peered through the railings. Myers's teammates turned away.

I staggered into the musty room and dropped to the ground. The sweat streamed down my body. My heart pounded over and over... I closed my eyes. The floor was cold beneath me, though the air was warm from the showers. I could hear my temples throbbing noisily in the stillness. A warm trickle curved along my lip line. Without opening my eyes, I grabbed a nearby garment and put it to my nose. I knew it was beginning to bleed.

I could smell Myers's body odor on my singlet. In the background, I could hear the fans cheering in waves. I thought to myself... " I just pummeled the state champ. I knew I could do it."

It was the constant haunting of a dream. I tasted it in moments, but it left me restless. It left me gazing to a place I had envisioned since the time I was young. Never sure if it would ever come to pass, never certain if I would ever fully seize the day, if I would ever triumph over my own self-- the greatest opponent of all.

I opened my eyes to stop the stirring of my mind. The mat burn on my face was stinging with sweat. My hands shook in front of me, without my control they trembled. I tried to focus on breath so I would not think. The red second hand of a clock, fluttered. The precious minutes went by.

The announcer introduced the next weight class, and the crowds cheered in response. I couldn't stay still any longer. I couldn't take the hollowness. I knew what I had to do; I took a deep breath and lifted my aching body from the floor. Putting my gear back on, I placed my hood overhead, grabbing my jump rope I headed back into the noisy arena. There was a place in the corner, away from the fans and aggression. I skipped calmly, watching my teammates through the wavering bodies. There was no rest.

Coach and the guys were busting on each other and laughing as they approached the bus. After about five minutes, coach Muller did a body check and we were off. It was close to ten o'clock now. The roads were dark and desolate.

I took a tin out of my bag, packed it, and rolled some tobacco underneath my bottom lip. " Young, let me bum one of those." I threw my tin over to our heavy weight Micciun. His large fingers were like claws. " Dam." " I'll get you back." He tossed it back, much lighter then before.

Keith walked down the isle and looked at me. " Josiah, can I sit with you? Naville ate four bowls of chili." " I feel for ya bro… Did you eat any?" " I had a bowl, but it's all good an well." I moved my stuff aside so Keith could sit down.

Keith was one of our JV guys. I had met him freshman year, and worked-out with him frequently. By junior years our friendship had grown. He was one of the few people who actually listened when spoken to; He seemed to take every word to heart. I think that was the most precious part of who he was. Keith genuinely appreciated who we were: Rug rats… Young cannibals. He hung with us, and over the course of only a few years became one of us. We respected Keith as a wrestler, and as a comrade. He was not someone who had slick moves and some kind of reputation. Rather, a devoted old boy. Keith's chances at varsity were slim, but he never gave up. No matter how hard he was pushed. No matter how many times we tossed and turned his stocky body, he never backed down. He was admirable.

Over the years I began to trust Keith and love him, a brother. I had adopted him into my family, and cared for him as if he were my own blood. He was one of the only people I would share my heart with. I don't know why I did. Being honest with him helped me to be honest with myself. I guess everyone needs a friend. He was, and knowing him reminded me I still had a heart somewhere to be found. For him I am forever grateful.

48

" Wanna dip?"

" Umm... I don't know."

" Wut do ya mean ya don't know?"

" I suck at spitting."

" You, suck at spitting? Here, whack a dip."

Keith handled the tin in an aquard fashion, as if he were putting a condom on for the first time.

" Give me that thing."

Keith took an ant's shits worth and set the tin on his lap. By this time he had me laughing. " I feel like I'm corrupting the innocent." Keith smiled and almost swallowed his chew. " Oh, brother."

" So wut's up man?"

He tried to break the saliva, which was now connecting his lips with his spitter.

" Hold on. Umm I don't know not much? Wut about you?"

" I don't know, just thinkin a lot."

" 'Bout wut?"

" Mostly my pops."

" Well how's he doing?"

" He's doin all right, I can't believe it's the same guy I saw in the hospital a few months ago."

" That's good to hear Josiah."

" Yeah. I think by the way things are going, we'll have another year or two together." Keith seemed a little taken back from what I said.

" God's been good to us, I know he hears my prayers." Keith nodded his head.

The ride home was pretty quiet after that. It was a cold, December night. The guys were exhausted and the trip was long. I thought about my father, wondering if everything was all right. Nothing was. There were a lot of questions at that time. My trust in God, manhandled like a toy dummy. My emotions, dragging me down. My thoughts gone astray.

I walked through those next months just waiting for the storm to come. I was the only one left, lost in silence, damned in a cursed house with a lady I called Mom. Though I had forgotten my worst days, I was reminded of them every time I looked at her. The memories had turned to pain. It was torture! I felt betrayed by my God. Condemned to die, yet still somehow standing. Holding myself high and with perfect poise. (For this was part of her orders.) I was crumbling inside. Growing weak and weary. Falling...

Seeing the clouds in the distance, I smelled the rain in the air. In my hours of darkness I searched. Calling for my imaginary friend, Jesus. There was no one.

She was raping me on that voyage to death. She had turned me into her ideal. That person I hated, my own reflection.

I knelt before the cross that night and begged God for mercy. Nothing came, nothing changed. No angel flew to save me. But I had to believe even if there was no hope, no Savior, no God in heaven; If my faith failed it would be the end. And so I kissed the cross like I was supposed to, said my vows and promised not to be a bother.

The Opposition

Like a young, faithful platoon we plunged, farther and farther into the season: Through dual meets and tournaments, through the long hours of practice. Battling, our fears with faith, worries with grace, foes with friendships, all amidst the long winter months that buried the sun and paled our woes.

Sullen and winsome, fray but resolute, I walked into the County tournament mid season. With my teammates and coaches on my sides, victory haled our grace.

Their scales were heavier than ours, and tripped us up right from the start. We weighed in on Friday at around five, wrestled a few matches, and then weighed in again at around nine. The rest of the tournament held on the following day.

There were twenty teams, with thirteen guys on each competing. The matches ran consecutively on five different mats all day and into the night.

Blood.

Three of us had made it to the final round. Bud, Charley and I sat and watched the consolation finals, then headed out of the gym for break. Now, in the first seed position, I faced Kurts, a long rival from Rotherford. I had beaten him in the district finals the year before, but it was only by an arms length.

It was close to five o'clock when I returned back to the school. The locker room stunk; There was snot on the walls, and shit that rose to the occasion. My shoes were drenched with sweat and my warm-ups still held the heat of the last three matches. The aches and pains... Worries returned.

I walked slowly out of the locker room and fell on one of the warm-up mats. My body was bruised and battered. All I wanted was to be in bed, for it all to over.

I was startled out of my sleep by the testing of the buzzer. The doors were opened, and the people started filing in. Bud and I warmed up for a little while, drilling our moves and jogging around the mat. Though we had to sit back down after sometime, for our legs were too tired to hold us. Finally, the waiting was over. The lights died, and the wrestlers made their way to the edges of the mat.

I took a deep breath in, standing to my feet. A seasoned veteran now, this was my life. I had become a legend to some, but I had long forgotten what was it all for? The announcer began introductions. That night, promising the crowd.

Once again I took the steps that brought me to the center circle. Drafted to prove something to someone, exactly what, I did not know. I continued on behind the façade of a star, ready to burn out, ready to fade away.

" Your shot! Your shot!" Kurts and I had similar styles: both cautious and defensive on our feet. The match was racking. We locked up over and over: exchanging shots, attacking and counteracting, scoring and failing to score. Barely. He was stronger than I. My dieting-- a disease.

Our coaches screamed on the mat-line, throwing water bottles and knocking chairs, cursing each other when the ref wasn't in-between. Roggetti, the coach from Rutherford despised me-- the only stumbling block to his instant success. Veins popped from his neck. Over and over he screamed. Buzzing in my ear like an obnoxious fly.

The third period came. Score, two - two.

" Green chooses neutral."

"You fellas like grapplin on ya feet, don't cha. "

Ready.

The whistle blew and we started the last round on our feet.

" Come on Josiah! Get out of that crap!"

" He's tired." The Rutherford coach yelled. " Take him! Take him!"

I pushed out of the tie and circled. A banner waved in the stands. I faked a shot and sent him sprawling. Then, I lunged forwards with all my strength. He too shot at me. Our heads slammed together.

Down on one knee, my hands waved out in front of me. I couldn't see a thing. Kurts ran to tackle. Motion slow. Coach screamed. " Stop the match!" "Josiah's down! Stop the match!" Two officials jumped in front of me and caught Kurts. The whistles blew.

I tried to run back to the center of the mat, but ran in the wrong direction. Then, my legs gave way. A fallen hush.

My head was buried. Paramedics.... medical kits in hand. The ceilings spun in circles above me. Bodies came and went. And familiar faces came closer. I began to cry.

" Injury time." Coach looked back at me. " No tears Young. This is yaw match. Do you hear me? This is yaw match." Rogetti continued-on over Kurts shoulder. The ref walked over after about a minute and a half. " Josiah, how many fingers am I holding up?" I could tell by the voice it was Old Smokey.

" Three."

" Now how many."

I paused. " Two?"

The ref looked at coach. " Is it worth it?"

" Josiah, wut do ya want to do?"

My eyes landed on Mom. She was standing at the edge of the mat. Behind her, my dad and grandmother looked out with blank stares. My dad was holding his hip monitor in one hand and a booklet for the tournament in his other hand. I had a feeling it was open to the page my name was on.

It was the only match he had ever come to see. I wanted to make him proud. My teeth clamped shut. I stood to my feet. " I'm ok Smokey."

Norwood quickly taped a cushion in my headgear, and handed it to me. " This should help Josie." I walked slowly back to the center of the mat. The score, two - two. Fifty three seconds remained.

Muller yelled with a blood curdling cry, " It's not over 'till it's over!" I looked over towards dad. " It's not over 'till it's over." This one's for you.

The whistle blew. We circled back and forth ready to devour. The time on the clock ticked away. The stands were quiet.

Kurts shot, knocking my head on his way in. " Ahh!" I fell backwards. The whistles blew around us. " Josiah you alright?" Old Smokey said. I didn't give him a second look; I ran back to my starting line.

I waited for the whistle, remembering dad. I dug deep within my soul. I would not cower, nor would I turn away until fear fled from the face of destiny.

The whistle blew. I grabbed Kurt's head. Then, circling him to my right, I ducked his arm and shot high. All of a sudden the gym lit up. Coaches stood to their feet and screamed from the mat-line. I lifted him up, dropped my shoulder and took him to the mat. " Two." The crowd went wild.

There was eighteen seconds left in the match. Kurts jumped to his feet. I grabbed his wrists and drove him back down. His hands slapped the mat. The crowds cheered even louder. I looked up at the clock. There was twelve seconds left. "Stop looking at the clock and wrestle!" Coach screamed above the uproar.

Kurts tried to stand up again, but inspiration fueled me; I ran him out of bounds, pushing him into his coaches. The metal chair collapsed beneath them both, and they toppled to the floor. The refs ran over as I turned my head away.

The Rutherford coach flared up at me. " Back to the center boys." With six seconds to go, the whistle blew. I chopped Kurts's arm, picked his ankle and drove him face first into the mat. Covering his hips, I waited for the buzzer to sound. When it did, everyone in the gym stood to their feet and clapped. No one cheered, they all just clapped. It was something I had never seen before.

Old Smokey helped me slowly to my feet. As my hand was raised, I remember pointing one finger to the ceiling, and feeling the spirit of God run down my arm. In those brief moments I felt the traces of redemption. I waved my fist in the air and walked off the mat to the embrace of my coaches and peers.

That match was the last Dad ever saw.

Within a Still Reflection

The lights were bright that night, a miracle. Though, victory was a short lived dream. I had fought long and hard, but could do nothing to stop the dying of my soul. That quiet river.

Eyes closed. I could see the flashing cameras and fans... The numbers on the scoreboard. My body ached, and I was still; The bed soft beneath me. Until that night I had always believed that I would make it, but I had grown tired and near to defeat inside.

There was nothing I could do to change the past from the past or stop the future from becoming. And so I faded to the whispers of what life could have been. Turning to the dark roads for comfort, finding there were others like me. Lowly, shadowed and poor... departed.

$\mathcal{C}$HAPTER 5

The Awakening

It happened as if it were supposed to happen, as if someone were taking me by the hand, and showing me the grounds I had already walked on; It felt as if I had been there before.

There were irreconcilable differences between the vast devastation surrounding me, and what I thought to be true and real. Wounds that ran deep, past the delicate, amiable springs of life; The truth could not be excused. With the passing of the seasons, winter's cold winds and spring's displays of hope, my independence grew with vigor and boldness...

We walked behind Ahnia's house at about one in the morning. There, the river ran beneath the stars as we held each other, kissing and talking with quiet, unobtrusive voices. Ahnia was the most beautiful girl I had ever laid eyes on. When I looked at her, I would often touch her lips, her soft skin, to make sure I wasn't dreaming.

I had never fallen in love before. But in the short time I had known her, my heart was captivated, entrenched with the riches of her presence. I was empty when she wasn't there. I would think about her through the long days, counting the hours until we would be together again. She admired me as well. I could tell by the way she looked at me; She would always find a way we could be together.

Ahnia didn't need me the way I needed her. She didn't fear the day when we would break-apart the way I did. So I tried to hold on to everything we shared, and received the part she gave to me. Trusting the comfort I found in the security of her arms, I gave to her all that I had, hoping foolishly it would be enough.

" I love you." She smiled and ran her hands down my back. I whispered into her ear again, " I love you." By the way she looked at me when I said it, I knew she cared, but she was scarred and scared to respond. We undressed each other, laying naked like children under the breath of life. Both longing... this was all we had, and was becoming all we knew. As one we united.

As one our bodies moved. As one we fit perfectly, and breathed… She was my escape in that time. When I was in her my hell was gone.

" Nia, I hope no one comes walkin through here..." Ahnia smiled and reached for her Parliaments. " Do you want one?" " Yeah toss me one." We pulled the cover over us and cuddled, looking into the heavens, watching our smoke rise into the warm night air. Our bodies lay in unguarded tenderness, our hearts beat side by side as we thought things we never thought before.

I had never seen the stars shine, nor had I felt a love so true. And in midst of sorrow, the changing tides, I waved good bye to broken dreams, many more to come. I wished in a soulless well for a lifetime with her, wanting to never leave and never to let go. I held her; She was all I had.

In the distance I heard the church bell ring… Awaken somehow, to a division that had started years beyond. The tears felt from the eyes of my soul as I reached for what I could not possess- life, betraying the promise I knew so well. It was my choice. And I longed for the gift to have worth, turning to face the blue horizon. Turning from the hot, desert sun, with my shadow confronting me, I walked and wandered, farther and farther. Then, running against the winds.

The river ran in a delicate and precious way that night. I listened to her speak, although could not grasp her secrets. Unto the dawn we lay and slept and left the world behind us.

" You did what?"

Miles passed me a beer.

" I told you."

" You a liar? Swear to God?"

" Would I lie."

" Josieman she is hot as hell. You lucky bastud."

Miles went off...

He took a deep breath in and looked at me, " So how was it?"

" It was sweet. But…"

" Pss. But wut?"

" Never mind."

" Oh, you pussy whipped. Once you get a little you can't stop. Huh."

Miles had been dating Tara for close to eight months. He was in love with her, and I was falling farther. When we hung out with each other, things weren't the same. We used to spend hours laughing-- carefree in spirit, but our lives were becoming more complicated. Our hearts carried this weight, though it somehow didn't feel so good.

We made our way back to a hang out we called The Bridge, beating the rain by only a few brief minutes. (It was a common place to move parties when the woods were wet or when the cops were crawling.) The size of a small church, it arched some fifty feet above our heads. There, the light chased the shadows off of the walls showing urban-eyed gargoyles, names and faces sprayed on stone, symbols.

Miles and I kicked it by the fire with a crowd that was two years older than us; They had already graduated. I was nervous when I hung out with these kids, they partied much heavier than I had seen. Milking their forties between guzzles of Vodka and Rum. Between puffs and coughs of marijuana they spoke. I watched them pass a huge glass bong with a skull on it dressed like a joker. The weed was laced.

Uncomfortable. They were a bad crowd, and I knew it from the get-go. Miles on the other hand, had grown up with them; He seemed a little more at ease.

Almost everyone there was friends with Ahnia through Carmen, her ex-boyfriend. He happened to be sitting caddie-corner to me. Periodically, he'd glance in my direction. Nia and Carmen had gone out for three years, broken-up for a mere four months before I met her. They were each others first love, the reason why Ahnia didn't want to get wrapped-up again. I envied Carmen for I knew Nia still loved him. She would often visit him during the week; She said their friendship was important to them both. It bothered me, but Ahnia was impossible to control. So I excepted what they had, whatever it was, and took the rest as I could. (Played a fool.)

For a while, Carmen and I didn't make any eye contact. Perhaps, the wrong place at the wrong time. But by the peace offerings that came my way, in the shape of joints and bowls, barrels and bongs, I figured it was all right.

The gathering continued late into the night, and I got myself to laugh and converse with some familiar faces. More times than not though, I found myself alone, and about ten feet back watching it all. There was something more happening. I couldn't quite put my finger on it, but I could sense it. It felt like something was wrong, terribly wrong. I looked at the scene over and over. Like I was in a movie; This script didn't fit my character. They were a bad crowd, but I wanted in.

If I could only escape the way they did. It seemed almost too easy. I was had... a loose wire. These were the 'drug kids,' their title had a luring element of fear in its timber. They didn't care, nor did I want to.

The struggle went on inside of me the whole time I was there. What lay behind this darker side? I was scared and fascinated. Cooed with a black-lip smile; My gaze turned towards the moon. Raging in the amber, midnight sky the fire burned.

In the pale of the moon: Mouths full of smoke, spitting whiskey. We were smitten, and we were young. Trying to mask the moment. Trying to amend ourselves with the haunting of the past-- the iron garden's rust. A thousand rocks soared, forsaking all in somber delusion... to black... We sung our souls to sleep one last time.

Short Lived and Short-Ended

I looked out the window and watched the rainfall. It was common for that time of year-- near to the beginning of spring. Earlier that day, I had been groveling under the deck of my mower. From the living room window, I watched the water carry the grass away. Oil colored streams crept down my driveway. I lit a cigarette and watched the skies grow dim. Crying Buddha's *Angels* played on my downstairs stereo. I listened to the singer for the Cry scream what I didn't know.

We were into extracurricular activities by then. Kile Jones and Carson too, pioneers furthering their horizons, experimenting with these things called mushrooms. They would get them from Jones's cousin. Jones referred to them as 'Boomers.' Said they were magical, grew on cow shit and you ate them. It didn't surprise me; It had to come from Jones you know.

Well, I bought a bag from Jones, and figured I give them a shot. Nia and I were going to do them on the weekend closest, but we had been in a fight for the last two days, and I didn't care to wait for her any longer. Plus, I was too curios about these magical mushrooms; I couldn't wait any longer. I went downstairs, grabbed the bag, and brought it into the kitchen.

Kile said to eat it on a peanut butter sandwich. Supposedly, they tasted like shit. Go figure! As I placed the caps and stems onto the bread, my phone rang.

" Hello?"

" Hey what's up?" It was Ahnia.

" Not too much."

" Do you have to work today?"

" No, it's too wet to cut. I was just chillin. Wutcha up to?"

" I'm going to come over."

" Alright. Like right now?"

" Yeah."

" I would like to talk about things..."

" So would I. We'll talk when I get there."

There was something was wrong. I could tell by the tone of her voice... But those mushrooms, I couldn't get my mind off of them. So I poured some of the blue and gray dust onto the pile I had made. Slapping some jelly on the other piece of bread, I began.

When Kile said I was going to embark on a journey, I never thought it would begin like this. But Kile was right again. Just the process of downing these fucking things was a trip.

I couldn't really taste the mushrooms, but the smell of them turned my stomach. I washed down every bite with huge gulps of water. And if by chance I was reluctant to quench the exasperating dryness, I would gag in hick-ups that left a twinge in my nose.

I chewed until my jaw cramped and tongue went limp with fatigue. All I kept telling myself was, " PJ with crunchy peanut butter. PJ with crunchy peanut butter." It was like a monogamous moan in my mind. But I couldn't lie to myself any longer; The yellow word 'creamy' shown through my blinking eyes. So without further a due, I decided ignorance was best, and turned the jar towards the wall. Soon afterwards, stepping out on my back porch for a smoke.

I felt like I had surrendered to something unimaginable. I wasn't sure what to expect. Didn't know if I would even get off on them. But as the time passed, I started thinking about Nia again. I was worried; What did she have to say? The phone rang again, startling me. It was Luke.

Luke never did anything except for drink. He was a good old boy, a beer drinker at heart. He hated everything else.

" You did wut?"

" I ate mushrooms."

" Oh my God. By yourself, you crazy man?"

" Lu calm down. It's all good."

" Why you gettin into that shit?"

" Luke, deep breaths now... There's more to life than just beer."

" Sounds like you need a woopin Jossie. A woopin and a tall one." He laughed.

" Be ignorant."

" Wutch you call me."

I loved pissing him off.

" Lu are you still there, I think we have a bad connection?"

" Ha ha. Cows shit from an asshole. Listen, I have to return my tux at thu mall. I'll stop by to see how you're dowin."

" That's chill. I'll see ya in a few."

It wasn't but fifteen minutes later when Ahnia came over. I stood at the door waiting for her; She was so beautiful to watch.

" Hurry up your gettin wet."

" Hey hun." She kissed me on the cheek.

" Hey."

" Wut's up, you got me nervous?" We walked into my room together.

" Wut's up?" Nia paused for a second. " I've been thinking a lot lately. You have to admit, things haven't been that easy." I felt my stomach drop.

" Ahnia.... you mean the world to me. I hate it when we fight. You're the one that likes to fight."

" What do you mean? You think I like going through this crap!"

" You're the one that said a good fight now and then adds a spark to the relationship."

" Oh did I?"

" Chill. Stop gettin all pissy. It just bothers me when this stuff happens. That's all I'm trying to say."

" Then say it next time."

" Nia, your my friend. If it wasn't for you, I don't know what I'd do."

For the first time since the Counties I began to cry. Ahnia ran her hand through my hair. I covered my face in absolute shame. My father's condition was declining. He was now on a weaker chemo because his body was couldn't handle the amount needed to reduce the cancer. He was dying, and inside I was too.

" Josiah I don't want this anymore. It's not working."

" Don't do this please." I buried my head in my covers hoping it was all a bad dream.

" Josiah we're different people. We need to go our separate ways."

" No Ahnia! I love you."

" I don't want to get any more involved. I'm going to school in the fall."

" Why did you let it get this far then?"

" I'm sorry." Nia put her hand on my back and rubbed my shoulder.

How could I live without her?

" Josiah... Just let it go."

My world was crumbling. I couldn't let her go-- she was everything to me. Lost. The rain fell.

It was all happening again. How many times would I spin through these vicious circles? If God was sure to smash me down, then who the hell was I?

Embarrassed, feeling weak. I managed to pull myself together. The waves washed ashore.

" I need some air." I grabbed my cigarettes off of my dresser, grabbed a warm brew and headed upstairs. I could tell Ahnia was relieved; Caring for someone besides herself was not in her nature. Hearts had been tangled, and I guess I understood: 'Nothing lasts forever.'

She stayed and talked for a while, and like a guide on that cold-world tour she asked me how the ride was. " Feeling better?"

The time slipped by and things began to change. Ahnia made her way to the door, not quite sure what to think. While I sat on the couch hysterically laughing. On her way out, Lu came in. "Have fun," she hissed.

" Wut's goin on here Josie?" Lu's initial response.

" ... I'm out of my mind."

" You sure look it."

I put my hands over my face. " My God. Wut the hell?"

" So wut's up with her? You guys get into a fight or somethin?"

" Uhm... We broke up."

" Is that why your eyes are all red?"

" Uhm... I don't know."

" So is that's it?"

I nodded.

The rug beneath Lu's feet moved like water as he walked across my living room. I was mesmerized... " Josiah." Lu said between his swigs, " are you goin to be all right if I leave?" " Me? Yeah, I'll be fine."

He didn't stay much longer; His tux was due back at the mall by four thirty. " There's a beer down the drain," he said with a smile.

I couldn't sit still; I couldn't stay in that house any longer. I grabbed some belongings and the keys to my truck and went outside. It took me about ten minutes to figure out how to start that dam thing. When I finally did, the stupid thing wouldn't move. 'Ok, foot's on the pedal. I'm in gear..." It was like the hand of God was just holding me there. The e-brake was on.

I drove the best I could for about a block and a half-- my thoughts racing. Besieged. I had to pull over to calm myself. The elementary school was just ahead.

Under the Crashing Tides

Drifting... A song called *Colorado Skies* played on my old stereo. Life was suddenly sweet under the gray, spring skies.

I lit a Newport and watched the smoke rise in the still air. The chains on my ankles unbound. I was flying.

My imagination took me in places as the evening set in. The silence spoke and the earth and skies and creation sung in waves, awakening me and urging me to look forward beyond my shallow vision... There was a glimmer on the horizon.

I was intoxified and in surrender. The more I let go, the more I went under, drifting lucidly beneath the crashing tides. I dreamed without the future, irremissible past: A past which manifested itself in the depths of night.

I started up my truck and made my way up to the green pond. It sat deep in the forest, on the outskirts of town. A good friend of mine lived there, and I knew even in the state I was in, I could talk to him; He would understand.

The rain fell heavily as the music played with a euphoric synergy. The cars streamed by and left their lights hovering in my vision. I chained smoked my cigarettes, driving confidently through all I had known, and all that I had never seen or touched, heard or felt, ever before. I was then, perplexed and in tune. Finally at home, in a mystery of God and bewilderment.

All evil was gone. I was tongue-tied, wide-eyed and crazed, singing sweet good byes to the life I had known. The miles passed.

When I was far into the dark woods, I came speeding around a sharp bend. My headlights suddenly reflected off the eyes of a deer standing in the middle of the road. Frozen! I cut the wheel-- the back of my truck fishtailing. My arms swung to regain control. I slammed on the breaks, skidding to a halt.

My heart pounded, the smoke from my cigarette burned my eyes. *Colorado Skies* blared on my stereo: " Dreamed I was flying high above the trees, over the hills." My hands shook.

I looked out, the road was wet and strange. Had I lost my mind? Night faded to black again, and I went numb.

Above and Beyond

The guys continued training, devoted to coach and the program, while I roamed the town for adventure, partying with different faces in unfamiliar crowds. It was a few weeks later when I landed in the middle of a week-long party going on at Angel's house, one of my former teammate's. Angel had follow the footsteps of his older brother and was now a runner for the biggest derelict in town. It just so happened that he had scored a fresh batch of mushrooms that night.

We passed the bags around and washed the 'boomers' down with beers and vodka; We sat waiting on the back porch of the old farm house. After forty minutes Angel pulled out a bowl, and we past it around the circle of friends; It was the spark needed. Halfway through the next bowl, things intensified; The mushrooms came on like a swell.

" Ang, I'm fucked up." " Me three." We walked in the backyard on the moist grass. The trees stood like trolls with decrepit arms and fingers. The field in front of us vanished into the dark.

" Yo check it out," Ang spoke in another voice. I took my cigarette and waved it out in front of me, painting the air; The air was thick.

Crickets spoke. Shadows moved as the tree limbs blew. We walked down to a small brook. Water like a goddess. The night, cool.

" Josie you look nuts."

" Do I?." Dove

" 'Tis all good." (I'm sure it was.)

Ang and I walked across the old, wooden bridge, through an orchard and into the corn fields. The moon stood watch, guiding us...

It was an hour or so later when Luke picked me up. We cruised down to Myron Cage's house, music blasting, cool air whipping on all sides. I couldn't wait.

" Wut's up?" I yelled.

" Drinkin beers. Poundin 'em. You got to see Myron, he's freakin wasted."

" Ah shit. Where are his parents?"

" Their golfing in North Carolina."

" No shit? I'm startin to like golf after all."

The Catalyst

Luke's engine revved up Myron's driveway. There were cars everywhere, music and heads. I swaggered through the scene, peering above a pair of small, silver shades. I had changed, and the looks I received were a constant reminder.

I knew everyone who was there that night, and it felt good to be with them; They were old friends. I made my usual rounds, though it didn't take long before I was pulled aside.

Brook was gorgeous. Exotic: Her dark skin and catlike eyes were enough to make dead man rise! I would have loved to see her naked.

"Hey sweet heart," she said to me." Josiah, I've been waiting to see you."

" You've been waiting to see me? Huh. Wut's up wit you?"

She laughed, " Just Drinkin." She held up her strawberry wine cooler.

" Cheers."

Things began to get strange though... I found myself fading again, feeling out of my element. If I hadn't known everyone so well, I would have lost my mind. Thank God I knew them all.

I sat down on the steps and lit a cigarette. " Wut the fuck is going on?" It seemed like a simple question. She was at first taken by my assertion. I put my head down.

" It's all a big movie." I looked down the hall and watched the characters acting out their roles. I was sustained a step away and a step behind it all.

' Wut the hell am I doin?' 'Wut the hell am I doing hea?' Thoughts...

The scene changed. Brook lit her cigarette and smoked it as best she could. Others cheered in the background; Naville lost in quarters. He chugged the rest of his beer, standing to his feet.

' Wut is this?' Thoughts again...

" I'm goin crazy or they are?" Brook gazed away. " Totally."

I looked down at my cigarette. " You deaf or dumb." " Right." She blew her smoke, staring into space. " That's wut I figured.".

Behind me I heard a jolly chuckle. I turned around, expressionless. There, sitting on the last step from the top was a pleasant lad with orange hair. He was grinning. (Must have been listening all along.) "Total diss bra, I loved it."

Brook walked away as I soon stopped paying attention to her. "Who might you be?" the fellow asked. Hesitant at first, I introduced myself.

" Hi, I'm Josiah."

" Andy." He twinkled when he spoke.

Andy's attention shifted; He patted his pants with a frown.

" Where the hell did I put my butts this time?"

" Here. Take one of mine."

" No it's chill. I prefer Parliaments, the brand of champion's." He flipped a cigarette up and blew the tobacco out of its filter. In short, we made eye contact. His face lit up.

" Your pupils are humungous. Wut did you eat?"

" I ate mushrooms."

" No shit, figures. Now I know where you're comin from."

" You do?"

" Of course bra, but they don't."

" They don't? Why?"

" They don't know wut's up. Their fucking clueless, but wut are ya gonna do?"

" They don't know wut's up?"

" Look, they've created their own little world, their own little reality. They don't see because they don't want to see. Their scared to let it all go bye bye."

" Wut do you mean?"

He looked me intently... " The world is not real."

We looked down the hall into the kitchen. Naville was on his eleventh dog biscuit, grossing out the chicks for attention. Charley was yelling through the window, daring him to eat the dog shit from the poop box. " Only on special occasions," Naville bragged.

Andy looked back at me. He was like a big brother who understood. Having a kind smile, he spoke with the wisdom that gifted him so. He was like a big leprechaun. Yeah, that's exactly what he was, a leprechaun.

" Josiah, do you wanna puff?"

" Hell yeah!"

" Follow me then."

So I followed him upstairs to his pot of gold, for I knew my luck was yet to run dry. He opened the window and crawled onto the roof. I followed him, and waited as he shut the window behind us. " That's to keep the bugs out."

We climbed up to the next level of the house on a couple of broken milk crates, stacked half hazardly by the rain gutter. We shimmied down to the corner of the house. A few kids gathered together, and as the lighter sparked between them I began to make out the faces.

Sye was there, and a couple of other kids I recognized, but did not know. Andy intercepted the bowl and passed it to me. " Is this cool?" I asked. The kids nodded. " It's all good."

It became a trademark. At every party or gathering, or on mere doldrums' days there would be a circle. The pipe always made its way around and left us in a womb of contention. We scraped the streets for shwag in dry spells, and indulged in the kindest of times. I had found a groove among Andy, Keith and Sye, and we came together to help cope with the changing of our lives, to help ease the fear of the future and to run from the tumult of our pasts.

We sailed on uncharted waters, through perilous paths unseen. We escaped the grasps of the darkest times, though shattered was the dream. And without cares of consequence nor shadows of regret, we traveled to the heights so few had ever been. And with our faith in freedom, like ships on the sea we were released; We kept the wild sands of time from falling... Thus, became the nights of wonder.

CHAPTER 6

The Nights of Wonder

The coming nights were filled with the sounds of music; It was the only thing that could set us free from the rhythm of slavery. Keith would show up, bringing with him the light from the flame that continued to burn in his heart. He would scream in song, " I want to live. I want to live again..." His words spoke of the cry in all our hearts. He sang about flying and believing-- to him it was real. Prayers to us all.

He would bring us to tears some nights, on others he would lead us to ponder, and on others he would have us in hysterics as he improved lyrics to a catchy tune about Andy. There was one thing I did know, there was strength when we were together. It took four of us to complete the whole and because of this, we valued each other more.

Andy was the riot. A golden child, chuckles and charity, wisdom and peace. He was a lover by nature, from Ohio with twists of Raver in his blood. He would marvel at the scenery of hills and trees all the while 'liquid dancing' as he called it. He had the eyes of a deer.

Andy would always lend an ear. With kindness he would listen, with compassion he would console. With a Mountain Due in one hand and a parliament in the other, with glassy eyes and those little birds that you see in cartoons flying around his head, he would help you to go on and live another day.

Keith radiated with passion, so too wisdom, order, love and devotion. He, like the rest of us, was discovering the person who he was. Though not as desperately foolish as we, he committed himself to different groups-- more of an ecliptic type in that period. He would smoke with us in his varsity jacket, neatly clad and longing to be with his younger girlfriend. Later he would be drinking Budweiser with the jocks, with resin on lips that launched romantic nothings into her ears.

Keith understood fractions of what we were going through. While we grew up with dysfunction, financial difficulties and many sorrows, he was favored though didn't know it. He lived in the big house on the hill, in the rich part of town. Dad was a doctor, so forth and so on. But beyond the pleasant life that the Torrelli's displayed to the outside world, there were things missing.

Sye was the reflection of youth, full of yearning, quick with laughs; He kept our spirits high. He, like Andy and I, came from brokeness. With only distant memories of what life could have been, he held onto the little he had, fearing someday he would lose that too.

Sye's mother was fifty-three years of age when she had him, obviously older now. With the energy she did have, she earned money to survive and provide all she could. Her parenting consisted of handing her son five's and ten's for Mc Donald's as she sat in an old living room and watched TV through clouds of smoke.

I was a fuel, chaos and energy burning-- giving of light in twists of temptation. I was filled with respect for my brothers, though I embraced the fury and rebellion the best I could, claiming to know better. My radicalness and pride unhinged me downwards, quicker then anyone else. I was in ruins, but I was a breathing fire.

I was on a quest, I said it many times. Circles of delusion, exile. I excused my actions: a journey to apprehend God. This was my darkest hour. Though hope faded, faith did not.

These were the nights of wonder, and we raged until the given dawn. We saluted the stars as we roamed in lands fit only for fiction. Our desire for purpose and freedom perpetuated. Truth was an unattainable virtue, and so we flew to no end. Amidst this great conquest, abounding grace and mercy was the only answer to our safe returns home...

It was a few months later. I found myself climbing out on that same roof to find the guys. They were away from the crowds as usual. I had dosed on LSD and in search to find others who were on their way. I walked slowly around the corner of the house. About ten feet back, I paused and stood there staring at them. After minutes passed Andy caught my eyes and reeled back. " Holy shit! You scared the shit out of me Young!" Keith and Sye looked up. " Oh my God! Josiah!"

" Wut are you guys doin up hea?" They handed me a pipe. " That's wut I figured. Yo, I got somethin for yas." My treasure was buried in two layers of tin foil. Andy sparked his lighter. " Dam, where did you get all that?" " Can't say. But I'll tell ya this much, tonight is the night we live."

We sat back and broke down the half sheet. Andy put a couple in his mouth, and then looked over at me. " It's all good."

The acid didn't taste, but you could feel a sensation of your tongue like a dull batter charge. It made my stomach turn. I could already feel the others ones I had eaten, and the anxiety only made it more. My body was tingling, and my spirit-- scared. I left the guys and went back downstairs passed the party. I walked cautiously to the road, hopped on one of Myron's bikes and rode over to see Angel.

Cruising in the open night air... The smoke from my cigarette was warm in my lungs. I started to feel outside myself, a step behind my being. I pedaled to the top of the wooded hill. (One of the many that spanned the urban countryside.)

Angel's lights were out in his house, but his car was in the driveway. I walked around to his backyard where I found him hitting a bong and listening to Pink Floyd in the candlelit room. " Ticking away the moments that make up a dull day..." The words sounded in a fraught way.

" Pss, yo Ang." He turned his head slowly and spoke in a low, raspy voice, " Yo Josiah, come on in man." The door closed behind me.

"What's gowin on?" He mumbled.

" Nothing, just partying down at Myron Cages. You should swing by."

" Carmen supposed to come over in like an hour, we'll see what happens from there." Angel sliced a piece of hash and stuck it into a long, water bong.

Angel was different than most people. He was a loner, spun you see. Lost it before he had ever done a drug. We all knew it; You could see it in his eyes. People at school thought he was just another class-clown, but there was more to the story. A story only he could tell. He was a breath away from the realization of nothingness, and thank God, didn't care to notice.

I looked at him in that dim void. His face was mostly dark, though periodically within the candle light I got brief glimpses. His eyes were blood shot. He had a downhearted expression on his face, like the entire world had abandoned him... like he had lost the will to live. His life was being expended by the catalyst. It was his best friend and only means of unfathomable escape.

We smoked together and said our fair wells, hoping to connect later on in the trip. I rode over to the clearing that sat on top of the steep hill. Looking out, I watched the unwavering lights of the city, and those to north in constant motion.

I was out of my mind, unsure of myself and my whereabouts. I stared out, picturing places by my own house and pictures by Hill Top Point that were the same; But I was lost. My mind went around in circles, remembering people who I'd seen in the condition I was in. A picture of Kile ran through my brains. I recalled Angel's lowly voice, " Come on in."

"Where am I?" I spoke in a voice I didn't recognize. I held my cigarettes out in front of me-- foreign. My lighter set off sparks that danced colors on the air. "Oh shit," I thought or said, and listened to my far off voice. I couldn't feel the smoke or taste the tobacco. I just kept hitting my cigarette over and over again.

"I needed to get back to the guys." There it was again, that voice or thing-- that substance of formal irregularity. I knew everything would be fine once I returned.

A lost child, I made my way down the steep road. The air blew past my head; I gained speed. I was a quarter of the way down, when I noticed I had no breaks. I dropped my smoke and watched it trail-off in the corner of my eye. Pedals under feet-- I had no shoes on to break my speed! Faster and faster I sped.

The curb was a foot tall on the sides of the road; There was no possible way to turn off. Panic! My mind flashed back to the image of the deer, eyes staring at death. I heard the screech of my truck tires, now the whistle of the train down below.

The wind now howled in my ears, a demon ready to take my soul. I could now see the bottom of the hill where the road turned. There, the wooden arms which blocked the traffic of the train-pass, swung down in a red blur.

I couldn't tell if any cars were stopped in the intersection below, if they were, I was surely a deadman. I leaned in and whipped around the dark bend, inches away from the curb. In an instant, I smacked into the blinding lights of the train. Like a brick wall. I screamed and put one hand in front of my face. The train whistle blew and its iron wheels trumbled. My eyes closed. Silver

The arms of the traffic barrier were across the road now. I tucked my head down, closer to my handlebars. I tried to open my eyes, but the light was blinding. Screams of fright! Shiver of death in my spine; I wouldn't make it past the barriers.

Hallucination; A lifetime. I made it. Whipping down an open street, past the rest of the iron cars. Within them, melancholy faces gazed wearily ahead. They hadn't. They weren't as fortunate; Their pale expressions told.

I coasted nearly a mile then pulled into Myron's driveway. The guys were waiting there for me. Their cars were running, and ironically, the Floyd played on Sye's radio right where it had left off when I left Angels. " … The sun is the same in a relative way, but your older. Shorter at breath, one day closer to death."

Andy approached me. " Bro, are you all right?" Speechless and faint, I stared at him. " Josiah you look like you've seen a ghost."

" Have I?"

" Bro, you can't go that deep. You'll go crazy. Stay with us all right."

"Yeah ok. I'll stay witchus."

" The night's young. It's going to be all good. Chill?"

" Alright the night's young... Chill."

Shaken; I just couldn't get the picture out of my head. That ghost ride. Those souls in wait. I felt like it should have been me in that train... Given in. Trumbling...

Sye and I hopped in back of Andy's cousin's truck. (Timmy had come up from Ohio to visit.) Sye reached out, draping a cover over us, and we sped across town along the back roads of Foxhill.

I figured if I hadn't died before, it wasn't going to happen that night. Sye on the other hand was testing his luck, surfing with one foot on the roof of the cab and the other in the bed of the pickup. I urged him, " Sye getcha crazy ass down," but he was insistent on making me laugh. He crawled on the roof and made upside down faces through the windshield. Andy cheered him on and Timmy that crazy fuck wiggled the wheel. Finally, as we pulled up to the light before the highway, Sye jumped back down.

Sye pulled the cover back over our heads. He was a trip, one of constant entertainment. We lied there as he made hypothetical situations: " What if the police pulled us over, looked at our bodies underneath the covers...." Sye said he would stick his head out at them, make an obnoxious llama call and pull the covers back over his head. I didn't know llamas had calls, and I still don't. Like I said before, it was hypothetical. Humor to us.

Sye would make me laugh until I couldn't breathe anymore. Now I don't know if his ideas had some kind of magnetism, but in the midst of his comic relief act on possible police encounters, lights went on behind us. Timmy's truck, full of tripping lunatics, pulled over. By this time, Sye and I were hysterically laughing and there was no way we could stop. Our deep breaths and sporadic snorts, followed by silent giggle-shaking and Sye's whispers to "shut the fuck up," were happening underneath someone's bright idea to hide us like illegal immigrants crossing borders.

The lights flashed blue and red through the pores of the blanket. Andy's door opened. " Shh, you guys keep it down." Andy started walking away.

Minutes later I heard footsteps running towards us. Tony and Andy were cracking up. Andy threw a couple of bags into the back, and Tony took off abruptly.

Sye dug into the bags. Whip cream containers? I didn't understand. Sye put one to his mouth.

" Ya don't eat it. Just suck the air out. It's Nitrous oxide."

" Like whippets?"

" Exactly."

We puttered along the dark roads and got to Sye's shortly after.

" Wut the hell happened back there?" The car doors slammed.

" Tis all good." Andy flipped up a Parliament and blew the tobacco from its filter like he always did.

" The police were bustin someone else is all. It's chill."

Andy tilted his head back and blew his smoke into the cool, night air.

" Timmy almost got busted though. Got the wa-was in the middle of the dairy isle."

" I almost got fetched by an old hag," Timothy replied; His teeth were a fist full.

We made our way to the edge of the neighborhood, destined for Old Dam. There, we could tune in and tune out. We ran through the yards that bordered the woods, using the light that shown through the house windows to see. We made it to the edge where the path began.

" Where the hell is Sye?"

" Wut?"

" Sye, where is he?"

I couldn't see a thing. " I'll go back. You guys go 'head."

Andy and Timmy flipped on their flashlights and quickly got away from the property. As I came around the corner of the house I saw Sye standing in the shadow of a tall pine. "Sye?" He slowly looked up at me. Withdrawn.

" ...Sye you all right?"

He lifted his head as if to speak, but said nothing.

" Sye?"

" I use to run through here when I was a kid. Me and Bret did."

He looked back at his footsteps on the wet grass. I empathized with him. I truly did. For I saw in his eyes during those brief moments, something too real and familiar to deny: The longing to be innocent again. Faraway, held in the flight and madness his soul churned for answers.

I took Sye by the hand and pulled him away. Step by step I led him until he followed on his own. We could see the flashlight in the distance as we stumbled. The neighborhood faded through the trees, and we reached the others.

Together we walked by the river. Her song was soothing, safe, and sung unmistakably like a prayer; She parted the sea of danger. Soon, we came to the clearing.

Old Dam was different than I had envisioned. It wasn't a dam at all. Once perhaps, but the middle of the wall had fallen. The water passed gently over the planar stones forming a smooth falls.

Here, away from town, there was peace and quiet. We sat above, looking out across the running water. The trees swayed. We were transfixed, waning under the moon. Yet there was a calm and a trust we could feel in those woods. We were safe there, safer than anywhere else, even in our own homes...

Andy packed a pipe and handed it to me. " It's all good bra. You do the honors." The lighter flashed and through the visual dazzles, I saw an eye looking up at me. I flinched. " Wut the fuck?" Andy picked the pipe up and lit the flame. " Meet One-eyed Willy."

The bowl was set within the head of a one-eyed troll. " He's been with me from the beginning," Andy said through his well-defined chuckles. So we passed William around and around, smoking ourselves stoned and silly again.

We were in the middle of one of our discussions about the way things were, when Andy pointed downstream. There, twenty feet away, a fawn and its mother drank. We watched, awestruck. And when my eyes met theirs, I heard a voice ask why? I had no answer, and so I was caught speechless as my scornful heart and life of slow suicide were revealed.

In the reflections of that time, I see now the hope. Where once the child-shine in us had been stolen, I began to feel the mystery of love. And in the darkness of that night, the light could not be quenched, though our aching hearts thirst beneath the quiet stars of August. Where truth once lived open and real, it now lay heavily at my feet. Yet still and in rest, my eyes met

70

the eyes of that fawn; I knew I could go on. And as the cool air met the welled tears within me, so I stared into her eyes. Her mother cared for her and brushed aside the fear.

It was then I remembered there was a God. For no creature could have been so genuine, nor could a heart have been so tenderized by its touch, unless there was a love... a love far greater than I. And though our downcast, guilt-ridden eyes pleaded, we ran from everything that could bare testimony of truth-- the arms that would not let go. I could feel something embracing me in the quietness of the night. I knew from that moment's time, life could exist on earth and heaven after.

We continued through the motions of our doubt, a little less sure of the recklessness of our steps. The bowls steadily made themselves around the circle of friends until the bags were empty, and our lungs throbbed. Our dance turned to the sting and despair of coming down. The strychnine ached our backs and jaws, as we tossed and turned on the uncomfortable, dusty couches in Sye's garage. It was at the dawning when we closed our eyes and fell asleep-- before the morning's light could give way. Blindly gazing towards the horizon, we wished for the golden days, the days that were pure and filled with promise. Days that were made real by the idealization of our memory, never to have existed at all.

The weeks went by and things continued to change. We spent our free time wheeling and dealing, getting high and planning our next fix. We often talked about our experiences on the hallucinogens, quietly yearning for the time when we would drift into the world of oblivion.

Kile Jones and Myron's crew was the worst of them all. Their group was solely based on their drug of choice; Experiments with cocaine turned to frequent trips to Harlem. Within months they were addicted and obsessed. They cooked up their own crack after school, and the glass pipe passed between them...

Souls wore thin.

Shinuwa Lake

They were lost days, creeping behind us and never to be found again. We would never see each other in the same light as we did then, nor taste the sweet breath of day together, aligned, seeing eye to eye as if one. With every season comes the departing of another, a letting go from within. And so our spirits would soon be challenged with the tests of time.

We sat down at Shinuwa Lake, a sacred Native American grounds. It was there we would talk and dream, listen and learn, write and reason, sketch and squander our thoughts on paper or in sand, or on the air for the world to know our charge. By the water's edge we would lay our burdens down and bring our sorrows to openness so the stars could find them with haste, and the waves could wash them away.

We spoke of a different world, a different place-- a place where we had never been, but existed beyond our shallow lives. We searched ourselves and combed the sandy shores. It was all in a dream. A dream for a time. A time when we tried to rise. We felt like revolutionaries in a place of cowards and slaves!

Andy and I sat by the water and listened to the waves.

" Wut are ya thinkin 'bout?" Andy always paused when you asked him a question.

" Uhm... Forgot." Andy chuckled. " Oh, Keith and Sye. They remind me of brothers."

" Yeah, they do... We are."

" I think you're right bra. Josie?"

" Wut's up?"

" I feel things when I'm down here. I don't know. Been coming here for years now, but have yet to put my finger on it. It's like you look out on the water, and something comes over ya. Josie, when I look out there, I know there's gota be more. There's gota be more than this."

" We are left to wonder sometimes..." I wished had I more to say.

Keith and Sye walked up from the shore. Sye lit a cigarette.

" Yo, check it out." He pointed with a lengthy finger.

The four of us looked out across Shinuwa. The picture spoke a thousand words, words that were shy from our lips, to perfect for our mouths to ever form. We smoked and talked in a circle of friends, friends who delighted in the magic of time spent and in the simplicity of steps taken. Steps towards what we thought to be freedom. Steps away from a life disdained. The night was young, and the beauty it portrayed lay within the arms of the ephemeral. We wished in wells of forever, but never to face the coming days or face the world alone. I solemnly remember the anticipation of the year to come. We talked and created to disturb the silence of the air.

1994

It was our senior year, a year to remember. No one could ever have predicted it would turn out like this. The school administrators knew what was up from day one. The eyes that peered and ears that ease-dropped on our scene were all too real. The faculty hounded us weekly, looking for the tangible evidence to confirm the bounties of guilt that marked our attitudes, talk and sway. We drifted farther and farther like fugitives with nowhere to run, outlaws with nowhere to hide. We were poor and we were young, doing what we needed to do to stay alive.

Magic in the Pines

It was ninth period. Myron and I met in the bathroom to discuss our plans for after school--Psilocybin! When class ended, we met in the parking lot and headed over to Angel's house.

It was a Thursday afternoon. The skies were grim and illusive. We found Angel in his backyard smoking from his bong. (As far as I knew, he hadn't moved from when I last saw him.) Startled at first, he seemed relieved that it was us.

"Ang, you up for shroomin?" Myron rocked his head back, exhaling his smoke.

" Are you guys crazy?" Angel mocked. " Follow me."

We walked upstairs to the kitchen. Myron and I watched as Angel rummaged through the freezer, lifting up bags and vegetables and packages of meat. He pulled out a few dozen books of acid, neatly wrapped in tin foil.

" Angel you nuts? You put all that under your mom's pork chops?"

" She don't cook a lot," he shrugged. To him it was reasonable.

" Wutta those prints?"

" White blot... Beeves and Butthead."

" Do ya have any Pink Sunshine?"

" None 'round."

" Well, wut's under the broccoli?" Myron continued to question.

" Broccoli?"

" Right there!"

" Oh the mixed greens?"

" Yeah, whatever."

" That's more acid."

" Angel we wanna shroom today," Myron injected. "The last batch was dank as hell."

" I get 'em from the hand that grows 'em... Can't get any kinder then this. Follow me."

Ang brought us upstairs to his room. He quickly pulled some suitcases out of the closet. As he recklessly dug through them, he started taking out huge zip-lock bags. They were stuffed full of the kindest mushrooms I had ever seen. There was probably ten to fifteen pounds worth laying on the bed when he was through. I had a feeling there was a lot more.

" Take as much as you want. This one's on me," Angel's mouth moved slowly. Myron and I looked at each other, then simultaneously looked down at the bags. We knew it could only mean one thing ... We were going to get wasted! Stuffing our mouths with caps and stems, we ate quietly until our stomachs were full and spoiled. Then, we smoked a bowl and headed out.

The streets were busy with traffic, honking horns and smog the air was thick with indecency. " Ang, where we goin?" Our lives were in his hands. He pointed in front of us where storm clouds flashed in the distance. " To the pines."

Neither Myron nor I had ever been there before. On the far outskirts of town, it was known by a only a few. Angel drove carefully under the canopy of trees. The rain fell steadily from the skies, hitting our windshield when the trees limbs dispersed above. The poison slowly aggressed inside of me. A perilous freedom.

Angel slowed down before the trail entering the pines. The trees tunneled around the dirt road. An enormous puddle gaped across the beginning of the path the size of a small pond.

" Angel are you fuckin crazy. You' re not driven my car through that are you?" " Relax," Angel casually responded. We drove along the embankment so that half of the car was up on an incline and the other half in the muck.

The trail was rugged. Large puddles formed by a rather systematic root structure scattered precariously about. The tall pines towered above all.

Turning off the main trail, we drove down yet another. The small light from where we entered disappeared. Lightening and storm crashed around us.

I felt like I was riding on the waves of a dark sea. These were the hours when visions became real, and we danced in our rite of passage. On these ancient grounds we awoke to a new dawn. Here, many waters passed; The spirits spoke. We felt at home: welcomed and embraced, captured and drawn to odds.

Angel rolled the car to a halt. We lit our cigarettes, and Myron packed a bowl. Outside the rain still fell, but was barley seen. It was the only way I knew how to fly. Everything else was gone. There was no crowd that could call me back, no guardian that could plea my pardon. I had given up on the cold, cruel world. I would no longer be slave, garnishing the roots of evil... the very turmoil of my soul. My life until then, but an illusion in circles; I was going nowhere.

Myron remained content in the vehicle, while Angel and I wandered throughout the forest. The pines were planted in perfect rows. (According to Angel, a project for the World War II veterans.)

Ang ran passed me, down into a thicket of small maple trees. He disappeared. I started jogging after him, and soon found myself running faster and faster.

The wet maple trees splashed in front, hitting face and forearms. I heard Angel yell from in front. I screamed back. Raging. My run soon turned to a blinding sprint as we whipped through the forest. Inside something had awakened, and we were imbued with life.

Angel's white shirt in front of me-- he leaped the fallen timber. I screamed again, and Angel whooped. The brush suddenly cleared, and the woods opened. Angel was but a stone's throw away; I was gaining on him quickly. All I wanted was to run by his side the way we used to... Angel grabbed a tree limb and plunged into the air. He landed; We were head to head.

"Wut the fuck's up now Angel! How bad do you want it?" (The words of coach Muller.) His reply-- an insane glare. We were savage!

Miles passed. My nose burned in the cold. I wheezed and panted, but could not stop. I had lost my mind, but not my will-- the fire burned inside.

We ran in parallel stride as we once had done so many times before. The agony of defeat thrust upon the stone, and the thrill returned. " I can't stop!" he yelled. "Fuck yeah," was my reply.

Things grew strange around us, another dimension. The forest grew darker, and the lightening flashed overhead. We flew on the air. The trees spinning around us. The water dazzled on the floor. The colors of the autumn leaves blurred across my vision. My arms waved in front of me, blocking branches and falling rain.

Angel and I had been climbing a gradual incline for almost a mile. We came sprinting over the hilltop. The car was in the distance. Myron turned around abruptly to see what was going on. We leaped from rock to rock, hurdling stumps that crossed our paths. Angel veered off. The hill steeped, and I felt myself moving faster and faster. I slapped the trees to slow down, but could not. My legs stretched in front of me.

At the bottom of the hill was the main trail. Piles of leaves lined the side. Angel, who was now in front, yelled and pointed towards the mounds. I hollered back. For about fifty more yards we hauled-ass down the steep embankment. Then plunged off the cliff, falling through the air, crashing under the star-smothered sky... leaves burying our heads in cold wetness.

Panting... Sweat streamed, and drizzle fell from the gray Jersey sky. I remember how it felt like wrestling: The smell of the air, but one fire burned. The silent scream in my soul. No evening light. The loneliness like growing old. Faceless, colorless foe. The chill in my bones. The percussive throbbing of my temples... The lonesome wander, a weary haul to freedom's tangled reigns. The haunting of a dream.

On my Return

I showed up for practice the next day. Muller must have caught wind of it from one of the guys; He was waiting for me. "Young, I wanna talk to ya. The local papers wanna do a write-up. Talk about ya dad and how you're bouncin back."

" I'm not interested."

There was something about the way he said it. That look in his eyes, I had seen it before. There was a 'but.' I was a trader to him now, though I didn't know it at the time.

" Mule, I'm hea to roll, not rumble." " Well we won't push it, my respects." Muller gave me a pat on the back; The bell rang. We went our separate ways.

It was the first time I had stayed after school for months. The halls were almost too still. When I walked past the wrestling room, the smell of the mats turned my stomach. I put my hand in to see what the temperature was like, surprised to feel how cold it was.

I headed to the locker room and suited up for the practice ahead. A heavy lump formed in my throat-- my pride. Wishing instead to be with Dad... He was alone and dying now. I couldn't be around him for long; It hurt to see him in such pain. It wasn't right. I took a deep breath in, lifted my head from the hard, wooden bench and made my way back to the wrestling room. The guys had already left for their run.

I was alone there, suffocating almost. Feeling like I was sucking dust from a dried-up well. The rain fell outside.

Doors swung open and the guys entered. They were startled to see me. As soon as our eyes met they looked away. I tried not to let it bothered me. We had deserted one another, I guessed. I knew what they thought of me, no reason to make amends.

As practice got underway the atmosphere was solemn-- like someone had died.

" Keith?" He knew what I was thinking.

"I don't know man, this is how it is."

Stagnant was the air.

" Young," Keith whispered in my ear.

" Muller says you've hurt the team, and it's not best if you stay."

"Wut? Wut did I do?"

Keith shrugged his shoulders as if to say," You don't believe that."

I stopped and looked at him.

"Whose side are you on?" Pushing him with both hands.

There was no answer, just a blank, lofty stare.

I eyed Muller. He was pretending to read the newspaper. How many years had I served him? For what?

Viable Atonement

A couple practices went by before I could actually make it through a whole workout. It was a new approach, but it was better for me to be there. Being on the mat was better than being by myself. The practices were shorter now and more self-driven. I wasn't holding up the team, just pacing things, trying to get back on track.

Muller divided us into groups for a round-robin. I noticed the kids looking at me, conversing quietly. The JV's and younger wrestlers were asked to leave the room. It grew quiet. Uncomfortably quiet.

The battle would begin. It would be me verses them. For they hated me now, and this was their time to show it. The eyes in the room converged to our group. The others peered through the windows from the hall. Coach slowly stood up. Grinning in that particular way, "Are you guys ready to wrestle?"

Charley and I were first up. I had a gut feeling.

The whistle blew. Charley came charging at me. My heart raced inside. It was as if he had been waiting for that moment. Waiting for it patiently. He ran me out of bounds, pushing me until I fell off the mat." Back to the center boys," Coach wailed from the edge. The whistle blew, and Charley came at me with an unforgiving scream.

I realized as I tossed and turned, pummeled and tussled the guys, that things really had changed. I wasn't one of them anymore, and I had to pay. It was a viable atonement, somehow well deserved.

I wrestled as if my life depended on it that day. Stood up to them like a man. A survivor who would never die; They had forgotten who I was; No one would deny me.

It was third period the next day when the phone rang in the art room. I was quietly painting in the corner. Mrs. Williams kept looking over at me and nodding her head. I thought it was Dad for sure. Mrs. Williams put her hand over the phone, " Go see Muller."

Muller had prep time, and his classroom was empty.

" Coach ya wanted to see me?" I said from the hall.

" Have a seat boy."

I pulled a chair up to Muller's desk.

" Well, wut's up?"

" More than I anticipated. Did ya see the article in the newspapa?"

" Wut are ya talkin about?"

" Your bud Chris did a nice write up on you. 'Young returns.'" Muller chuckled under his breath.

I smiled, but I did not own it, shaking my head in disbelief.

" Muller, I'm not."

" I told them not to get carried away with it. Lighten up."

I lifted my fallen eyes up to him. " Is this fun for you?" But the words did not come out.

Betrayal never tasted sweeter than it did to him then. Coach would use me whether I liked it or not. He had his agenda.

"I don't want it to be like this," I told him.

Muller lifted a Styrofoam cup to his mouth, letting a mouthful of tobacco juice run down the inside.

" Anyhow," he continued. " Shapiro and I were looking at the Christmas tournament and..."

" Wut?"

" Well, we're gonna need ya."

" Muller I already told you, my dad... I'm not."

" Hey, I've had hard times too. Took me nine years to graduate college. Sometimes we have to put our own personal cares aside. The team needs ya. We could win this..."

I almost choked myself.

" But Muller, I've only been on the mats for a week. I'm not in shape."

" Sorry boy, suck it up." Muller put his head back down.

I returned to the art room, isolated behind my canvas. My hands were trembling. ' Is this really happening? How could this be? The team will hate me if I let 'em down. I can't.' Mrs. Williams walked up and knelt down beside me.

" Josiah, I think you should do it." She was a mother to me.

" Mrs. Williams," I said. " With all due respect, stay out of this."

" I think you should do it."

Her words echoed in my head.

The tournament was a day away. I still hadn't stepped on a scale since the last year, but I could tell by the fat on my face I was five pounds over. The scale read exactly five.

Charley walked over and put his sweat gear next to my locker. " Your gunna need this." I spent the next three hours running and skipping rope in the showers. The other guys practiced lightly and rolled out around four thirty, except for Charley. When I realized he hadn't left yet, I asked him why.

" Waitin for ya... Wanted to see how you were doin there with your weight."

" I'm light. Do ya remember how their scales are?"

" Their the same as ares. I think the one of 'em is lighter."

I grabbed my towel and walked towards the shower.

" Josie."

" Yeah, wut's up?"

" Wanna chew?"

" Yeah, I could go for one right about now."

Charley threw me his tin.

" Still chewin the pussy shit huh."

" Josie hold on one minute." Charley walked into the coaches' office and grabbed a newspaper.

" Here we go, old times."

So we sat in the back of the locker room, spitting into the drain like we always used to. We hadn't talked in a long time.

" Your class is pretty weak this year Josie."

" Is it?"

" Yeah, this here's the year remember."

When Charley spoke those words something died in me. My eyes skimmed over the county lineup. The further I read, the more I realized what Charley was saying was completely true. We were at the top now.

Minutes had gone by before I lifted my head from that paper. As I caught Charley's eyes, I noticed he was dearly troubled. " Bro wut's the look for?" He glanced down towards my hands and then looked away. My hands were shaking. " Char it's cool. I haven't cut weight for a while."

Charley and I were like brothers, it was true. We had been in each other's corner for almost a decade now; We had seen each other win and lose. But when he looked at me in those minutes, I felt for once like a different person. Like my true self had died, and now in front of him, a cheap imitation, was all that was left. I could see the hurt in his eyes, like he had been robbed of a friend.

In all the years I had known him, through all the ups and downs, he had never seen me like this before. I was falling: I was frail, and I was weak, and I could tell it scared him. We finished our tobacco and went our separate ways. Knowing inside that we had come a little closer, in the midst of growing worlds apart.

Wilkshead Tournament '94

My alarm clock buzzed at 5:45 a.m., and I rolled out of bed. My muscles ached from the long hours I had spent making weight the day before. A lone wind howled outside. I pinched some tobacco from my tin, and rolled it under my lip. *Hopeful Skies* played on my alarm clock radio.

I packed my bags knowing well and fine it would be a long day ahead. I can recall like it was yesterday, Eddie singing those lyrics-- " He who forgets is destine to remember." Resonance. Hopeful Prayers of the Skies

Outside, a thick frost covered my windshield, and a light snow fell from the weary sky. I drove cautiously down Terrace St., watching out my window for Charley's car. I would have given anything to see him that morning. We used to always pass each other on the way to school.

By the time I got to Washington High, the bus was ready to roll. " Lets go Young!" Muller yelled out the door.

We all made weight like we were supposed to. It was early in the season still and no one was sucking out yet. The tournament started around nine thirty: First they ran the preliminaries, followed by the first round, which started around eleven...

How I did it, I do not know, but I made it to the semifinals. My legs were tired and my chest ached, my head pounded, but I managed to go on.

" How do you feel?" Shapiro questioned.

" Like shit."

" You look it Young."

He squeezed some water into my mouth; I walked onto the mat. Old Abe the ref, looked at me reassuringly, " Good to have ya back Young." I waited for Nelson in the center. He was bouncing in his corner, staring at me with a piercing intimidation. His coaches stood around him.

" Lets go red. To the center." The ref motioned from the tables. The auditorium was getting congested with people now. It was nearly three o'clock. " Lets go red!" The ref demanded.

Nelson sprinted to the center of the mat, slapping my hand. " Wrestlers ready. Tables ready." The whistle blew.

Instantly, we locked up. Nelson squeezed my head, snapping me up and down. " Get out of there Josiah!" I drove Nelson towards the edge, then snapped his arms. He fell forwards, and I clubbed the back of his head with my forearm to accelerate his fall. His hands slammed the mat.

He jumped back up to his feet, infuriated. He ran towards me, grabbing my head to tie up. " Watch the throw! Watch the throw!" My coaches yelled.

Just then, his hips dropped down below mine, and his arms whirled around me. I went tumbling, feet kicking high in the air. I slammed on my back; The wind knocked out of me. "Uhh."

Nelson cranked my shoulders down... inches from the mat. His coaches and teammates screamed, "Deck him! Deck him!" I could see the ref in the corner of my eye. I could feel Nelson's weight on top of me; He was overcompensating. I let him begin to turn me, then I rolled him through and out of bounds. "Back to the center boys." But I could hardly move, gasping there for air. " Green, you need injury time?" " No." " Lets go then." " Top man ready?" The whistle blew.

I had nothing left in me: muscles weak, lungs closing in. Things around me grew faint and surreal-- almost black at times.

" Up off the whistle Josiah! Up off the whistle!" I clamped up. His coaches yelled, "He's stalling ref, he's stalling!" The ref slapped on the mat. " Bottom man you got to wrestle." The clock ticked from forty seconds down..

" Bottom man warning." There was a roar from Nelson's side. The clock ticked... the buzzer rang.

Nelson bounced up; I knelt on the mat trying to catch my wind. ' I can't go on,' I thought. ' Its over.' The referee tossed the green and red coin. It flipped around with a slow motion, hanging definitively on the air. Landing on the edge of the mat, it rolled a couple of feet, and then fell to its side.

" Your choice Young." " Defer." " Red?" Nelson pointed down. " Red chooses bottom." " Lets go Nelson he's tired! He's gassing out! Beat him!"

Muller and Shapiro sat quietly in my corner. People entering the gymnasium, now gathered around. Nelson's teammates filled his corner, reminding me that the odds were not in my favor. I had lost it.

I signaled to the ref. " Top man optional start." The whistle blew once again; It left a ringing in my ear.

Nelson cautiously stood to his feet. Then he turned and pummeled in, reaching for my head and arm. He scooted his hips to throw me. " Toss him again! Toss him again!" His hips dropped, and his arm clenched around my head. My body tossed around and I landed with a dead thud; He knocked the snot out of me.

I had never heard so many people cheering against me at once. In those brief moments, I saw people from my own team eager for my downfall. I could no longer breath. Warm blood ran from my nose to my chest. Nelson squeezed harder. Finally, the whistle blew.

I slowly stood to my feet. Defeated. I held my hand out to shake his, but then realized the match was not over. It was only the end of the period. I turned towards my coaches.

Muller had walked away. Shapiro wouldn't look at me; He kept his head down as he played with a piece of dirty tape. I was ashamed.

We started back on our feet again… Things grew faint around me. The screams turned to monogamous moans. The dream then silenced. Tears fell in my soul. I reached for nothing.

" One more huh."

" Yeah one more," I replied.

Keith threw me his shampoo from across the showers.

" Josiah, a wins a win…"

" I guess."

" Are you all right man?"

" Yeah, I'll be fine."

Keith smirked.

" Keith, keep it up. I'll kick your ass… Owe this fuckin mat burn!"

" Josiah, I can honestly say, I don't see that happening."

I limped out of the showers, flushing the urinals behind me.

Keith shrieked like girl, " Owe my balls! You're such an asshole!"

" That's for laughin at me."

" You fagot! You freakin burned my balls!"

" Balls? I bet your gonna tell me you got a penis in there too."

" You're a dick!"

" You're bein a wiseass. Hair Pie."

Keith had been nicknamed Hair Pie, and rightfully so. He was a small, little man, supposedly having some ape on his dad's side. Either that, or he hadn't quite evolved with the rest of Homo Sapiens. I personally found the former to be less likely out of the two theories. But over the years, I had heard good arguments on both sides.

" Half man, half orangutan. That's no joke."

" No, not an orangutan, an ape." Charley boasted; He had a knack for science.

" Shh, shh… it's all about spelling errors here he comes." Voices quieted.

Keith walked onto the bus with a childlike innocence. He looked around a couple of times, then walked down the isles. But as soon as he made eye-contact, he knew. Half of us were ready to burst out laughing. Some of the others, who had a little more self-control, kept their poise.

" You guys shut up. You're such dicks! This has been going for four years now. Josiah, I'm sorry for making fun of you."

" I don't know... ya didn't seem very sorry before." Keith started cracking up.

" Owe holy shit! Get this kid off me!" Charley held a wad of Keith's legs hairs between his fingers.

" I need samples so we can decide once and for all Hair Pie. Besides, you shouldn't be wearing shorts in the middle of December."

" It's not my fault Naville dried his ass on my sweats."

" Naville, wut I tell ya 'bout doin dat?" Boner giggled.

" I'm sorry Bone... It just happens sometimes."

We hadn't laughed like that for years. It felt like old times again. The bus drove down the quiet avenues. Christmas lights blinked through the darkness of evening's fall. It felt like Christmas time.

I packed my chew and passed my tin to Keith.

" Hea ya go."

" Thanks. You have a spitter?"

" No."

" Can I share yours?"

" I don't want ya dribble all over it. Hea just use this."

I handed Keith a coffee cup.

" Will do."

I thought about my pops a lot that ride. I already missed him. Christmas was soon to arrive, and I was without a prayer.

The bus pulled back into Wilkshead around six-thirty. We climbed back into our singlets and warm-up, tied our sweaty shoes and walked slowly to the grandstand. Most of the wrestlers were ready to roll.

I felt alive.

The announcer began welcoming the spectators. Reporters lined the sides of the mat. Cameras flashed. " Josiah." I turned. It was my mom.

" How's Josiah?"

" Fine."

" What's a matter witt you?"

" Nothin."

We looked at each other eye to eye. The announcer began introducing the weight classes...

" I got to go."

I stood within it all again: The thrill of victory and the agony of defeat, where legends were born.

I tug deep in my soul that night, wrestling with all that I had left within me. Crowned a champion, I stood there with grace and humility on the fractures of my dreams. With tears in my eyes. Counting the moments; They were all that I had.

I watched the remainder of the tournament through the small panes of the hallway doors. It was there I was befriended by a priest named Father Michael, a miracle above all. He would become a friend who would stand by my side. Lay his life down on my behave.

In the days that followed, I began talking with Father Michael and would visit with him every chance I could get. We would speak of the troubling waters at bay, of divinity's gaze from the distant shores, of flight and of sorrow and of poems that could be sung with reverence beneath the blissful stars in winsome skies.

Shadows on the Horizon

As the glory of that fine day faded, the aches and pains soon came. I had pulled a flexor muscle in my hip during the finals of Wilkshead; Woody told me to stay off my feet until it could heal. Coach Muller didn't want to hear it.

It wasn't but two days later when he called me down to his office. When I got there, he quickly shut the door behind us.

" Would ya like a chaw," he asked.

" Thanks."

" Josiah Young. The name's got a ring to it, doesn't it? Like it means somethin."

I took a liking to what he was saying, though it didn't feel right.

" I have a favor to ask of ya... son."

"Wut's up?"

" We got Oak Ridge on Saturday."

" Yeah, I know."

"We're going to need you."

" Woody said not to push it."

" He's bullshittin. You'll be fine." Enough was said.

That match put me on crutches. I was down at Woody's icing every day. He tried to tell to me, I didn't understand. Muller had it in for me. He kept putting me out on the mat. They wrapped strips of rubber around my hip and thigh to hold my leg in place, and sent me on my way.

Disgraced.

My team watched from the sidelines as I fought for my dignity and my honor-- something that I could not let go of. It was then I realized I was in this thing alone.

On our fifth duel match against Verona, I was taken down, but never made it back up. That day was the end of my wrestling career.

Paradise Lost

" There's one thing that comes to my mind when we talk about God, Jesus Christ. Thank God for Grace. Please open your hymnals to page 121. We will close this Sunday's services with *Amazing Grace*." Father Michael and Father Elsa walked down the aisle. The alter boy held the crucifix. Families quietly made their way towards the doors. Doors opened and light shone in.

" Father Michael how are ya?" " I'm doing well thank you." I scurried behind some bodies and headed for my truck. I wasn't in the mood to talk that day.

" Josiah." " I stopped dead in my tracks." " What happened, why are you limping?" I wanted to cry. " I got injured Father Michael." " How? What happened?" I shook my head. " Josie call me. Promise?" " I'll try."

As I approached my truck, there was that statue of Christ. I found myself still in my tracks. I limped towards it, eyes set. I cried from within. Tears welled. The confession of my soul, " I've lost."

The loneliness of that day was beyond words, and so I kept to myself. The skies were heavy and gray; I longed beneath them.

Christmas in a Cold World

I knew something had to be true as life ticked away; Something had to be sacred. It was hard to believe in a God; It was hard to believe in anything at all. And during Christmas I was reminded of this-- so much missing. I sat and wondered what life would be like if there was a savior: One that really answered prayers, healed the broken, rescued the hurting. One that could make this nightmare go away. Was I ungrateful? Would I be forever left?

Dad would cry out at night. His pain was real, and I could feel it every time I closed my eyes. He was growing weaker. I tried to think of old times, times when I laughed and drank the sorrows away. I thought about coach and the team. Charley, who wouldn't speak to me anymore. All the lost years...

Sometimes I wished I could end it all; I was not brave enough.

Home was a strange place-- a place that would never change. I walked through the busy mall, people were everywhere, but I was more alone than ever. In a small jewelry store, I found a locket that was divided into two halves. The inscription read: " Lord watch over us, while we are apart from one another. Genesis 31." I bought it as a gift for Dad.

On Christmas Eve, I knelt beside him, holding the chain in my hands; Dad noticed that I was wearing the other half. He lifted his head from the pillow, and I clasped it around his neck; He rested his weary head. I kissed him, " Merry Christmas Dad." He replied, " Merry Christmas."

The peace that, that night was supposed to bring, never came at all. As I looked out from my window, I yearned. There was sorrow, lost love.

Winter's Cold

Day after day the clouds masked the heavens. Day after day we did all we could do to laugh, all we could do to get away from the dreariness surrounding. The winter was bitter cold. Colder than any other I had ever known before. The snow would fall, but ceased to melt away. And the precious sun became like a stranger.

The Bible above my bed had grown dusty. The cross, which once held so much meaning, became meaningless. I lost my will to live.

The ashes of my cigarette fell as I closed my eyes and listened. Keith's words were echoing in my brains: " And so I'm left, looking out my window. I think of things I should not know, and somewhere shines the pale moon light. God protects those in the night. I guess the world's outside my window, but I 'm happy here to let it pass from me. And mother, please don't wake me in the morning. It's a tragedy I do not want to see."

Gray Stone

It was a divined night, and we possessed its essence. Everything seemed so familiar to me. Dashavo you might call it. Andy, Sye, Cortney and I drove through the windy back roads of Foxhill.

I knew I was closer. To what, I could not determine; The journey waged. We had dosed on LSD exactly an hour and four five minutes earlier. I could always remember the beginning...

Sye's house had become a known hangout, open to many. It wasn't rare to find rave kids and skaters running with the preppies, or the earlier crowd there. Nor was it unusual or strange to see them getting along in such great numbers. We were not the only ones who squandered our time on such misguided dealings!

By early evening, Andy and Sye had landed a fist full of acid; The print, Pink Sunshine. Different than most, it was said to be clean and specially potent. It was ten o'clock p.m. when we dosed. Though, I vaguely remember splitting moons of ecstasy before then. (We had an appetite for destruction.)

It was a sure thing, if we stayed we would have been disavowed without remorse, missing our chance to explore the realms of the unimaginable. So we put the house in the keeping's of a few good friends, leaving the scene shortly after.

It was eleven forty-five. I watched the iridescent clock in Andy's car blink. 11:46. The batch we had attained was in fact strong and clean. (Clean-- a play on words or just me?)

" Hun, take one a mine... Hello in there?"

" Josie." Cortney held her New Port in front of me.

" I got my own."

" Umm... you look like your having a bit of trouble."

" More trouble than it's worth," I tittered.

"Give me ya light."

I watched as the lighter sparked in front of my eyes. The smoke hung in the dense air with a greenish glow. I dragged my cigarette. Smoke filling my lungs, my head fell back. The heroin in the ecstasy came alive; I was overcome.

" Keep the shit down when you pass it." One of Andy's rules, he didn't have many.

" It cool. No one comes back hea," my dissidence.

Cortney leaned over me, rubbing her breasts against my side; She grabbed the bowl from my hands. We were high, and our perceptions were hazy-- feelings and thoughts mustered. A car passed. It seemed so far from anything real. Headlights hovered in my clouded vision.

I could tell Andy was trying to keep from going under. He was driving. I didn't know how.

The signs that came, came and went without our knowing. It wasn't until we drove around one peculiar bend: We were in Gray Stone.

The moon struck us all by surprise, startling us from our slumbering dazes. The clouds rolled by as that pale angel, a mediator between the living and the dead, sat watch above the institution. " No shit. You got to be fuckin kidding me!" Andy spoke for us all.

Keith was rather fascinated with his cigarette. I watched him waving it back and forth with the music. Laughing at him under my breath, " Henesie. You're an addict."

Andy suddenly stopped the car and fumbled with the stereo. Then with a proud grin he smiled back at us, giving Keith, his copilot, a cool nod. *The Lunatic* played...

" Ahh shit, what's up now?" Andy proclaimed and took off driving towards the main gate of the premises.

Before us stood a sign that read, " Stay Out Violators Will Be Prosecuted." Andy killed the headlights, and we rolled slowly passed the gates. He turned the tunes low so they could barely be heard above the crackling gravel. In my mind flashed an unsettling image: A patient stood in front of the car with a moonlit gaze. His face was shadowed, cheek bones ribbed with white. I shuttered, then came to.

It was cold and desolate on those grounds. The moon at half mast. I flashed back to a scene from *The Wall*-- the character banging on the rock with fists of blood. Dying to come back, he had sealed his fate.

Andy leaned out the window, looking at a map of the property. We drove forward again.

" Wut's up?"

Andy kept silent.

" Do ya know where we're at?" I did not anticipate a sure reply.

" It's like a maze back here. Don't think we're lost."

" Wut do you mean? "

" Nothing bra, it's all good."

" You sure you can get us outta hea?"

" Do I lie bra?"

I let that one slide.

" Well someone do something," Cortney retorted. " Seriously, I don't want to get busted. I'm already on probation."

Andy continued turning about the gravel roads.

" That's the same map," Sye pointed.

We didn't understand what he meant.

" Here." Andy handed his pipe. " Pack it up."

Old Willy was a little older now. His head would actually pop off from time to time. But we reckoned it was a good thing; He had a tendency to 'resinate.'

" Right there. That's the same sign," Sye pointed.

" We're driving in circles!"

" Shit." Andy slammed on the breaks, and our bodies lunged forwards.

We screamed.

Andy thrust the car into reverse, flouring it back down the road. The car wove from side to side, kicking up dust from the shoulders. He stopped abruptly in front of the sign; Clouds of dirt rose before the headlights. Andy killed the lights and got out of the car.

We were lost, dancing with the devil in the pale moonlight... My fate-- the institution on the hill. A shadow rocked before a window.

" Keith, those curtains?"

" What? Where?"

" Right thea..."

" Oh my God. It looks like a person."

Lights went off in the building. Looking back towards Keith, I noticed a person standing in front of the car. The one I had imagined earlier; He was staring at me. My heart started raising. I opened my mouth to speak but nothing came out...

" Andy get in the car you moron!" Keith laughed and rolled up the window.

Andy clumsily jumped back in the car.

" I'm losin my mind..." Whispers from inside.

" It's all right bra," Andy stated. " I'll get us out of here."

" Dude! Dude your rolling!" Keith pulled the e-brake; Our heads jerked.

" Andy, where are we?" Pilot talk.

The rest of us sat quietly.

" We're fucking lost." Cortney murmured.

" No we're not. Stop with the bad vibes. The sign had an arrow that said, ' You're here.'"

" Moron wut does that tell us? Your so stupid."

" Chill bra, I'm dumb... Maybe just happy."

" God help us," An old oak tree creaked.

" Shh! Did you guys hear that?"

" Bra if you fart, I'll kick your ass."

" Shh! I'm serious."

" What ?"

" Forget it." Keith replied.

" But the sign says we're here?" Andy insisted meaning.

Andy took out one of his parliaments and blew the tobacco from the filter. His lighter flashed. Headlights shone it the distance, blinking between the trees. I thought I was hallucinating at first, but Sye confirmed.

" Shit, car!"

" Oh shit." Andy patted his jeans.

" Where are the keys?"

" Oh my God, you didn't Andy!"

" Look outside did I drop them? They have to be somewhere."

" They're in the ignition you moron!" Keith reached over, starting the car in gear. We lunged forward, then stalled out.

By now the car was coming right for us-- headlights shining in our eyes. Andy started the car again and whipped us around off the road and then back. Turning the headlights on, he floored the engine. " Go! Go!" We yelled at the top of our lungs. Andy sped forward in a rage of panic. His eyes beamed in the rear view mirror... " Shit it's a pig?"

I saw the steep turn through the windshield, trees waiting for us on the other side. " You can't make the turn! You can't make the turn!" As soon as those words had left my mouth, Andy did the unthinkable. He killed the headlights.

We rolled through what seemed like eternity. There was nothing but blackness. The tires rolled noisily on the loose gravel. Then silence. Andy cut the wheel, and we slid towards the passenger door...

" What's up now bitch?" He yelled through chuckles that sent his Parliament bouncing." Sye looked up, " You made it Dog!"

We turned amongst the side streets. Andy had saved the day! He chuckled to himself, securing our safe return.

Later that same night, Andy and I sat together. His poolroom was chilly and musty. Outside, it began to snow. We watched from the old, dirty window overlooking his driveway.

The snow barely dusted the earth. The trees stood motionless, their tall arms reaching into the skies. From time to time one would sway just slightly, but enough to stir the still, quiet hour. We had little to say, and so we listened, listened to that which was forgotten.

Lone Day

" It's nine o'clock now, beep him from Seven Eleven."

" That's chill."
" Wut flavor are ya gettin?"
" Pinacolatta."
" I don't think they got Pinacolatta Slurpies at this store."
" What flavors do they have?"
" Cherry and Coke."
" No banana?"
" I don't think so."
" Wut about blueberry?"
" I don't think so bra."

Andy sat at the light, and we waited for his car to move. The light turned from red to green and back to red again.

" Decisions, decisions."
" All right bra. Cherry it is."

The outdated, navy-blue Ford Escort puttered along the quiet roads. The speedometer never broke the 20 mph mark. It never even got close. Our eyes were blood shot and minds were fried; We had been smoking weed nonstop since four in the afternoon. By then, our only hope was a brain freeze. Not only did it help to preserve the brain cells, but it was a pleasurable experience .

" Owe my freakin head. Dude, if I crash because of this brain freeze, I could sue."
" You're high. You could never get away with it."
" No dude. I'm stoned."
" Right."
" Hey, ya never know bra."

Andy slowed the car down.

" Josie, what do ya say we head over to Boners. He's havin a party tonight."
" That would be trippy."
" Beer."
" Yeah man beer," we imitated.
" Fuckin beer dude."
" Beer, beer, beer!" The little car swerved along with our cheers.

We approached the noisy house. Dazed of course, though very perceptive. We entered through the back door, wandering amongst the crowd. Voices raised in the dining room where the jocks and cheerleaders guzzled their drinks. The quarters bounced across the table, dinking into shot glasses and smacking into beers.

Boner stood up, and with the yell of a constipated warrior he commanded, " Fuckin drink motherfuckers!" Some chugged, while others started singing a copella, " Here's to brother Boner the worst of them all. He eats it. He beats it. He even mistreats it. Here's to brother Boner the worst of them all."

" So how's Josiah?" A familiar voice, one I had trouble placing. I casually turned.

It was Debbie, Debbie Flanegin the class slut.

" Oh hey, how's it going?"

" I'm so fucked up right now... Yeah, I just need to lie down somewhere."

' Bad pussy always comes easy,' I recalled the words of the wise.

" Drinkin a lot of beer huh."

" Wine coolers," she held one up. "I love getting drunk."

" All right then… Andy help!" Andy stuck his arm up across the room so I could see him.

" Stay away! She's psycho dude!" He shouted through the crowd.

" Whatever," She rolled her eyes.

Andy and I made our way into the kitchen, quite amused with the crowd.

" Bra, I haven't been so entertained in months."

" Yo check out Naville." We wove our way through the bodies.

Naville looked like he was praying to the gods. He lifted his head up slowly from the table like a meditating Budda. Everyone started cheering, " Lets go Navi!" Before him leaned a tubular hunk of brown matter.

" Josie wut the hell is that?" Andy's face looked like a mush-mash pie.

" It's a can of dog food."

" No shit."

" Not yet at least."

If you remember, four months prior he was entertaining his groupies with dog biscuits; He had obviously graduated to bigger and better things.

In that time, Naville was extending the 'getting psyched episode;' The period before the unveiling event. This is what he loved to do. The longer he kept the crowds, the more he felt loved. A rather silly fellow!

Andy tapped me on the shoulder. " Here trade places, I can't watch." The party was growing louder and louder. The street was getting congested with drunk souls; It was quite the place to be.

" Josiah! Josiah Young, wut du fuck's up man?"

" Miles hey."

" Fuckin aye! Haven't seen your ass in a shit load of time."

" I've been preoccupied."

" Preoccupied. Pss, damn mutha fucka. Hea drink a beer and live long!"

" Sure Miles, give me a beer," I laughed. It was the same old Miles.

Nodding our heads, we looked on to the living room once again. It was that time. Time for the Willy Wilkins skit. The moment we had all been waiting for.

The beer cans went flying everywhere as Boner stood up, all two hundred pounds of him. " Willy Fucking Wilkins!" He roared. Half of Naville's crowd flocked over from the kitchen. Others began pounding the table in anticipation of what was to come.

Willy was a long rival of Bones'. Having beaten him in football and wrestling, now all Bones could do to seek vengeance was get drunk and shout obscenities from twenty miles away. At the height of his act, he would begin crushing beer cans on his head. One time I watched him recycle almost ninety. He would get so wild-up it would take four or five people to hold him down. Sometimes he would get so 'deep in the zone,' he would pick out random victims to actually be Willy Wilkins.

" Willy Fucking Wilkins..." The crowds cheered. " Senior year, me and fucking Willy Wilkins." After Boner's normal intro, which looked onwards to a future come back, he would break into the Slim Jim commercial and mimic Randy Macho Man Savage. (A pro-wrestler from the eighties who made an extra buck doing Slim Jim advertising campaigns.) I guess Bones didn't have enough original material.

" Higher education got you down," I whispered to Andy.

" Wut?"

I nodded towards Bones, " hea it comes..."

Bones held his fist in the air, " Higher Education got you down. Snap into it, Snap into a Slim Jim."

Every one cheered and toasted. Bones tore his shirt from his chest, and began to flex his monstrous pythons. " Snap into a Fucking Slim Jim," the drunken voices yelled in celebration.

" Lets go smoke a butt man, he's gonna blow." We left just in time. Bones was eying out a drunken sophomore who was halfheartedly humoring him. Marking this unfortunate one as Willy Wilkins... Willy Fucking Wilkins.

" Fucking Willy Wilkins, man I miss that skit. Andy go to the back porch so we can get some air."

" Chill." The sliding glass door opened and shut...

Soon, Boner came out staggering.

" Fucking aye dude. When I heard you guys were here I came runnin. You guys catch the act?"

" Yeah, very nicely done."

" Thanks man. Now let me feel your beers."

" You wusses. You know what you guys got to do?" Bones grinned.

" You need to take off your skirts and strap on some dicks. I mean take off your dicks and strap on some pants. Shit! I always fuck that up. Take off your pussies and strap on some pants. Fuck! You know what I mean right? Now take a beer and chug it. Just like old times. Here wait a minute, let me finish the rest of this. All right one for yous and one for me."

" Ok Bones on three... Snap into it!"

" Yeah. Lets do it... One two..." Then someone yelled "Cops!"

" Oh Shit!" Bones went running in to his house, and the rest of us ran out. Andy and I drove off into the sunrise.

CHAPTER 7

Speaking With Angels

Seven p.m. Tomas, Cortney, Sye and I had all eaten acid. It was a double-sided print; Space ships on one side, stars and stripes on the other. We had dosed on two and a half hits each, unaware of the potency of the chemical. We were used to the shit Angel Carson was dealing, that was the problem; His batches were watered down and duplicated for maximum profit.

I had sat in with Savage and Jones times before; They had many philosophies, many methods of mind expansion. They insisted acid was more than a drug. "It was far more powerful," they said.

Savage would crawl around in the grass of his backyard during the wee hours of the night. He said he would get so completely lost, he wouldn't know where he was or how he got there. I myself had experienced similar phenomenon. Savage said it was the dream world. The state of oblivion, where your thoughts become reality.

"Alien blood"-- this was one of Jones' theories. I snickered to myself. What had become almost a religion to Jones was no longer; He had, had a radical conversion. I had seen him in the beginning of that night...

I had been waiting for my ride at Charlotte's Web, a local restaurant where I had been working. A car came speeding around the corner with a hub cap flying. At first glance it appeared to be an old police car, but I soon found out it was Kile Jones. He skidded to a screeching halt, and I saw a white object bounce from the drivers seat to the stirring wheel and then back again. I hesitantly approached.

" Jones, that you?" The white object rotated, and underneath I saw a dim silhouette of Kile Jones. " Jones why are you wearing a motorcycle helmet?" " My mom crashed my car, that dumb bitch. I'm fucking pissed." The light turned green and Kile Jones sped away. The side of his car was mangled from front to back. That was the night of Kile's 'incident.' It turned out he was driving over to Savage Daily's; They had a trip planned for two.

We had heard of people having bad trips before, but never knew what was behind it. Kile Jones had become the exception. His only words about that night were, " Do you know wut it is to have total faith in God?" Kile Jones was an atheist. I didn't really understand.

The sounds of the Floyd prophesied: " The sweet smell of great sorrow lies over the land. Plumes of smoke rise, merge into the laden skies. A man lies and dreams of green fields and rivers. He waits 'till the morning with no reason for waking..."

Those words circled my brains...

Entrenched in overwhelming emotions, I was going under and farther than I had ever gone before. My endorphins were triggered by the acid; I began to see my soul separate from body. Everything around me became like a pattern, energy cells.

Jones had explained, whether an abstract rendering or literal truth I didn't really know. " It's like stopping and smelling the roses." He had said, " The acid permeates every part of you, and forms a thin layer between your brain cells. Your electronic pulses jump between cells, causing a gap in time..."

My arms flowing, moving like a flower on ocean waves, weaving through, tracing the currents of timelessness. I noticed a cold sensation on my cheeks-- tears that had been streaming down like rain. I had not blinked; I did not care if I would ever close my eyes again.

The air was liquid thick. I sent signals to my brain to move my arm, then watched my body move... Like water on glass covering the sun, the trail hung motionless in the air.

This was the avenue, the space between the conscious and subconscious mind. Where spirit world and the physical became one. The rest remained unspoken: everything and nothingness, hope and peril... life and death infinitely met. And so I entered that place without any warning, and with little knowledge. If it were not for the guardians by my side, it would have been my last night on earth. The digital clock read nine thirty. I watched and waited for it to blink another minute by, but it did not. I waited even longer; Time was then still. I grew uneasy. There was a familiarity about this place. Like I had been here before and knew somehow that I would return. I was in the womb where I had started, but I had prematurely returned; I was an intruder. I had broken God given laws. Guilty.

I was terrified-- struggling. My hands and legs were weak. Sounds of the Floyd, " The silence speaks so much louder than words of promises broken." Promises broken... I tried to focus on something else, but my thoughts could not stand in light of truth. I was dying.

The clock had not changed-- nine thirty, still. I looked into the physical plane of existence, what I had once called reality; My fears manifested. Cortney turned to me, " Josiah do you want a cigarette?" A distraction, anything, but as I reached my soul was torn. I was not hallucinating; It was real. The life I had been living was the illusion. I could see through it all, the lies... To you I will not lie!

I had overdosed on LSD. Kile Jones was right, you couldn't physically die from it, but you could mentally. He had chosen to leave. And I? I was prematurely witnessing my fate. The end of existence.

A young man named Caine was at the party, he turned to look at me. With blazing eyes that sent a shiver down my spine he mimicked my very words, words he had never heard me speak. (Whatever was controlling him positively knew who I was.) " Trippin dude? How's the trip?" Cold.

There was the devil. I knew it well and will never deny-- that demon possessed him.

" I gotta leave." I got up and started walking. Caine turned to me, " You're going to crash and die." His blatancy, night. Everything stopped around me. Silence, but a heart beat.

I sat back down, conversation resumed.

Framed before me like a movie screen, a perfect microcosm of a world... Cortney and I sat on the other side, eternity behind. I was in judgment, at the will of my fears, watching my fears enacted in front of me. No one else saw what was happening, nor did they know they were being used. Like puppets on strings they were dangled, blind, undercover... Something so much greater.

" So anyway," Cortney professed. " Yes?" " Are ya sure ya don't want a hit?" No." I don't." I could breathe again. Sane.

Tomas sat across the room. He looked over at me with a certain confidence. There was a familiarity about him, a twinkle in his eye I couldn't quite put my finger on; I seemed to have known him. He could see what was happening. He was like Courtney. I could see light in her eyes, but was yet to trust my intuition.

I slowly stood to my feet again. Caine turned to me, " You're going to die!" My heart dropped into my chest. Back down.

Defeated, weary yet struggling there and then between life and death for eternity. Terrified; My hands and legs were weak. I hung on that hazy line...

" Besides all of that..." Courtney glistened. " Should we continue?" " Is there a choice?" She looked over at Caine, her face darkened for a moment, " There is another choice." " No," I replied. " Let's continue."

I shook.

It was on a fierce hunch I made it to where I was. From a desperate search for something good, something right and something true that I had ended up there, at the dead-end of a wrong road. If I were to go any farther, I would have to check my body at the door. Kiel Jones had chosen to; Insane! Now his words made sense. I understood...

I was confounded with truth, for I had given in to a slow suicide. The demise of myself; The absence of God. No life. No tomorrow.

The evil dragging me down by nature of my being. Why? I swallowed poison. Justified.

Seeing death and believing... I looked out across the smoky garage one last time. Those who had been with me... No more... No nothing!!!

I gaped at Courtney, " No!!!"

She raised her eyes. " What do you mean?"

" I don't want to go! Not now."

A dark whirlwind was drawn into a cloud of shadows.

Courtney's luminous eyes held me," What do you mean?"

" I love my family..."

" Sarah won't make it without me; She needs me."

And...

" And dad needs my help. He's dying."

" Why have you quit?" Her eyes, gentle.

I could see the church in my mind: the prayer walk, the green grass, tall oak trees. That sacred part of me remembered...

" I will stay."

I was spared-- bound by a greater good, grace. The storm soon pasted.

Later that night when only Syed and I were left, he took out an aged guitar and began to strum. " This is a song I wrote. It's called *Heaven*." His eyes closed...

The room was still a haze, static on a TV screen. Smoke lingered, but the sound was pure.

" I know the way you feel inside. Don't cry. I can see right through the color of your eyes... I'm in heaven, here on earth with you, and I want you to be strong. I'm not giving in, and we won't be here for long..."

Dissention

These hours started off much like the others. I remember driving under the overpass smoking Mike's pipe, that old proto-pipe. It had a resin catcher and an extra scraper built into it. I believe we had just been at the park. It was a school night, so I had to be in by nine-thirty.

I walked quietly into the front door as Myron pulled away. My breath and hands stunk like smoke. I knew if I could make it past mother I would be fine. I quickly jogged up the stairs passing my dad and my mother's reflection in the picture window; She was still grading papers. " That you Josiah?" "Yeah, it's me."

I leaped up the second flight of stairs and darted into the bathroom. The mirror was an honest reminder of the toll my lifestyle was taking. My eyes were bloodshot, and bags hung heavily under them. My skin looked weary and malnourished. My cheeks were drawn and muscles had withered. " My God," I said unconsciously. " My God."

Downstairs my father began to moan in pain. Stark cries. He had been unconscious and was coming to.

I walked down a couple of stairs and stood, watching him in that hospital bed. He was dissolving. He weighed about eighty-five pounds. His skin was white like a ghost's. His dentures would no longer fit into his mouth, and his tongue searched the dry air. His blue eyes screamed. What was to be? His body had become like a transparency, only a trace.

I watched him still and from afar, with fear in my eyes. I could not help but ask-- How could life eminently come to this? Horror.

Dad began to come to, squirming in bed. " Rosie." " Rosie." My mother walked over to the bedside. " Josiah come here," she said to me.

We held my dad's hands. He tried to speak, but his body was so lame, he could barely form the words. He tried harder but still nothing would come, an anxious struggle. His back arched and his arms pulled at the straps that bound him.

" Mom undo the straps. We have to get these stupid straps off of him." " Josiah, he'll pull the intravenous out." " Mom get them off." We tugged and pulled at the white canvas straps.

Then, a calm came over him; The expression on his face changed.

" I'm back on earth."

" What Thomas? We can't hear you."

" I'm back on earth."

His words were clear to me, though mother didn't seem to understand-- hidden behind a veil.

" Rosie, I loved you."

She pretended not to hear him this time.

He continued, "Vanessa, I love you so much."

" Sarah and Roane, I'm sorry. I love you."

Then my father looked at me. His eyes were blue. Every voice in my head stilled. " Josiah, why do you do that?" " Wet the fuck do you mean?" I screamed inside. I was speechless. Scenes from my life flashed through my head, right up until that car ride home-- I saw it all in a breath. With a slight pause, he then looked up at my mother. " I'm back on earth."

Lasting of Time

The next months were painfully slow. For some reason dad didn't just leave. Month after month he continued to hold on and fight. What was he possibly fighting for?

Courtney and I drove up the windy road to the green pond. Her family lived by the water.

" You're quiet Hun."

" Sorry, just tired."

" Is everything ok?"

" It's all good."

" Well, do yam feel any older? Your birthday's tomorrow." She lightened the air.

" Yeah, I feel like an old fogy. Shit."

"Yak don't look any older, just a little grumpier."

" Funny."

" Hun, you know I love you." She did.

That night Courtney's family celebrated my birthday. Her sisters had bought me gifts, even her little sister Kimberly. They were family to me.

Courtney and I lay close that night; It was good to hold her. The cool air gently blew in from the window. I could almost hear the rustle of the waves from the shore. It felt safe there, a refuge away from the storm.

That morning the phone rang; I was woken. Courtney's mom informed me that it was my mother; I needed to go home immediately.

Somewhere inside I knew Dad was gone. I was angry at the world, and it hurt inside. Roane and mother were there waiting for me when I returned. They informed me that Dad had passed on during the night. It was my eighteenth birthday, a day I would never forget.

Three Days

The wake was barren and colorless. A black family reunion. I sat in the big seat in front, for no one else wanted it; I couldn't bare to see it empty. I heard the normal comments: " He looks good," " It was his time honey," " It's a shame," and there were a dozen, " I'm sorry's."

Sarah sat in the second row by her boyfriend. She loved my father dearly. It was hard for her, like I, to see him go. I wished for her to find some peace, but there was little; She sat quietly.

Venesa and Reane stood within a circle of guests towards the back of the room, carrying on. Their laughter was disturbing, spiteful. Things were different for me; I had learned from dad's failures, though it didn't seem like enough. I looked away, wanting only to bring homage. " Thank you for the long haul, whatever it means."

There were many people who came to visit on that day: teachers and students, athletes and coaches from other towns. My wrestling coaches came as well. It bothered me too see their faces, especially coach Muller's. His acts of pity were of no recompense. A grumble of solidarity.

I had no words; I remained quiet for three days. And on the third day, I walked like a soldier in black towards the shoveled hole where a mound of dirt lay. I set Dad's casket before his headstone along with the others. That somber day. I tried my best not to cry. No one knew him. Though, I had seen his heart break. I had watched his struggle day after day-- his fight!

Father Michael was there that day. I can't express how good it was to see him; Nothing mattered to me more.

As backs turned, I finally broke down and wept over my dad's casket. My tears fell on the cold, black surface. A surface that mirrored the skies above; I know he saw me from heaven. I stayed there for a long time grieving, baring my soul. It was too soon to say good bye; There was so much left unsaid.

My charm dangled, and I wrapped my hands around the cross he had left behind. My hands were wet with tears-- they trembled from all those that I could not cry. In the distance the breeze blew amongst the budding trees, almost too far away to notice. I could still hear the words, " From ashes to ashes, from dust to dust." Why did it have to be?

A Summer Close By

It was one last desperate plunge, with no artistic benevolence nor songs to brighten the hours. The innocent in our laughter had waned, and what we once excused as mere curious tamperings had become a way of life; The path was worn into the fabric of our beings.

We no longer used substances unless they were deemed "hard." We were strapped to them, and left to dance in their worthless highs and lows, throughout the dark-iron wilderness. How we prided in their lethal touch! The smell of mint leaves makes my stomach turn due to the mass amounts of PCP we smoked that summer.

There was a time when we sat around a kitchen table close to four hours smoking dust. We didn't get out of our seats until the bags were kicked. By that time, we could barely walk. The bags were saturated with the oil. Those mini zip bags were so wet Savage would smoke them when he was coming down. We nicknamed it "Diesel." "Big D!" It was like a whippet high for hours and it kicked our asses on many occasions.

There was the time we got lost in the Seven Eleven for forty-five minutes. The poor Hindu thought we were crazy. It was soul-threatening madness. I could hear the warning bell; It sounded like the buzzing power-lines by my house. I would remember the sign on the fencing that read, 'Danger Keep Out.'

We frequented the line between life and death that summer. It was no longer a high; We got a buzz at seeing how close we could come to dying. There is a door. I've knocked on it before. Coming to end is a fierce realization. A terrible revelation. I could hardly breath... Felt like an anvil resting on my aching chest, pinning me down and leaving me there to squirm and flirt my limbs.

We had other favorites besides angel dust. The ecstasy circulated still, but it was better to do with other drugs. With acid it was called 'Candy Flipping.' With Special K it was called another night. Special K was the name given to horse tranquilizer. We were a bunch of asses who needed to chill the fuck out, so I guess it was legitimate to use. We were able to get our hands on a few crates full of the shit. (I don't think the veterinarian minded. The window was open anyway.) We had dozens of vials. A quick, twenty minute bake in the oven, a little chop-chop scrap-scrap and it was ready to go.

Yes, and there was the bittersweet relationship with crystal meth. A drug that left you a crack-head on the city corner. I would shake and shiver and think of all kinds of fucked up shit. I couldn't even look at myself in the mirror, but yet I would do more. I always said it would be my last time, yet I had no will to turn from it. I had no strength to say no, like I was its fool; It consumed me.

I never have a drug of choice; I did whatever I could get my hands on. I would hang out with whomever wanted to get high. I was a junky, plain and simple.

Jones's group was probably the worst of all. Their coke habits turned to massive crack use. It left blisters on their hands, which soon turned to calyces. By the end of the summer they were shooting heroine. After a while I stopped hanging with them. I was no better, and preferred to be no worst. The summer of 1995 turned into one big relapse that left me broken. I was shattered like a crystal vase on a hard, marble floor... left swirling.

Over and over the darkness besieged me, though grace called me home. Finally, I decided to get out. I sold my business and used the money to go off to college. I had saved since I was twelve, and I guess it was worth the sweat; It got me away.

I pledged myself to start walking the right road again. It was steep, and I would get lost in the landslides, but I was moving forwards and towards the light. I could see it from time to time, shining above ground into the deep whole from which I climbed. Every now and again, I would wander over to a jagged edge, and just gaze off. Only would I see, the shady valleys from whence I had come and the stone... miles and miles of stone.

Stroudsdale University, PA

Nov. 1, 1995. My phone rang around nine o'clock p.m. I had dozed off for a short while on my desk. The obnoxious gangling of my roommate's phone startled me.

"Yo."

"Josie, it's your boy, wut up."

" Andy, wut the fucks up!"

" Chillin. How are ya bra?"

" I'm all right. 'Bout yourself ?"

"Chillin. Yo listen things went down this weekend."

"Wut are ya talkin about?" Things grew quiet.

"Savage overdosed on heroine."

"Wut?"

There was silence.

I had seen Savage snort double lines of cocaine as long as his hand. I had cleaned his puke when the dope would overthrow him. The only overdose for Savage was death itself...

" Is he alive?"

" He was pronounced dead, but they brought him back. It's chill bra."

" That fuck!"

"Needles bra. It's all 'bout needles."

Andy said a lot of disturbing things during that conversation. " The death wish was spreading," he had said. That particular line just stuck out in my mind; I didn't really understand until I went home.

Death Wish

It was a Friday night…. I don't what it was, but as soon as I crossed the Delaware River into Jersey, a feeling came over me. I just knew I shouldn't have gone. The roads were dark and shadowing. I guessed Andy was having a lot gatherings at his house these days. Why, I didn't know.

There were ghosts there I tell you. Living ghosts with familiar faces. Some I could barely remember the names of, others who I knew and loved. They were all ghosts now.

Their skin was pale and white, except for dark circles under their eyes. They talked in strange, unfamiliar voices; It wasn't them speaking. It was the demons clothed in the skins of my beautiful friends. There was no fight left in them.

" Andy wut the hell happened?"

" It's the reign bra. The reign of the king."

" Andy, speak English."

" Dope bra. It's all 'bout the dope now. It's him."

"Who? Wut are ya talkin about?"

"Evil bra, it's him."

Andy put his head down. He had every reason to, because he was right. It was the devil, the prince of the air, and he dangled my friends around in cheap costumes, by thread too thin to see. Just toyed with them-- no regrets or regards.

I asked Andy a lot of things that night; A lot of things he could not answer.

" Andy, why are you in this scene? Your betta than this."

" Josiah. Do you see them? They're me. I'm just a pussy is all. Too scared to go on, to stupid not to turn back."

" Andy shut the fuck up! That's bullshit!"

"No bra, this is wut's left. This is all we have. I need them, and they need me right now. Josie, ya know how it is."

I did know, and I was the last one to talk. I had made it out, but I didn't know for how long, or if I would be able to keep walking away.

Cortney came that night. Her beauty too, had vanished. Her eyes were sunken into her head, and she bugged around with the rest them. Andy told me she was prostituting herself in Newark, lived with a crack dealer named Rock. " She was strapped to dope," he said.

Sye and Andy used to hold Cortney at night. All night long they said they would wait with her. When I heard the resentment in their voices and questioned why, they said she shook so hard, if they didn't hold her she would fall apart.

Jones, Savage and Myron were all heroine addicts. Angel Carson-- crack head. He got locked up-- killed someone on the way back from Harlem. Andy said he couldn't wait to 'dip his bag.' Never the same.

Keith was ok though. Thank God someone else had made it out. Good old Keith couldn't give a rat's ass about anyone but himself, but he seemed all right. Just smoking the kind buds up in Boston with a bunch of yuppies!

So many lives were over though, over before they had even begun.

Desert Shores

I returned to school. The year would be harsh and trying; I struggled with addiction and all that bound me, taking steps forward, but sleep walking back. I thought being away from my friends and family was only going to temporary; Little did I know, memories were all that was left. I'll never forget the quietness... the stillness. It almost took my breath away.

Everyday was a battle to stay alive; Suicide the greatest temptation of all. The voice of a thousand lies haunting my soul. I imagined my funeral: Confused friends, the desperate moans of family members. I held on, though I wished I could end.

Prayers before bed, brief and to the point. " Save me..." I believed God was hate, and I was a disgrace. In the deepest part of me there was a hope though. I knew life was somewhere to be found.

When Rains Ceased

Still breathing... I lay in bed thinking about the place we would visit when I was young. A log cabin we used to stay in, fields and mountains all around. My roommate, Whitney, whispered from the bottom bunk. " It's gowna to be all right." (I used to tell him about the place I dreamed of, before I slept.) He knew what I was thinking.

" Josiah, where do you think it is? It's in your heart." " It's a dream," I told him. " You should follow it, maybe dreams come true," an epiphany shy.

Good-bye Cold World

On May 26, 1996, Whitney and I left for Colorado. The sun shone on that Sunday in an old, precious way. We left in the evening from Whitney's house, across from Philadelphia. The Chevy van Whitney had bought from an auction was packed to the brim. With clothes, food and furniture, art supplies and snow boards, and whatever else we could fit. We drove off. Sun set.

The trip was long. It gave us plenty of time to think about all that we were leaving, all that we might never see again. I know as we looked out that dirty van's windows, we were trying to envision what our new lives would be like. For Whitney it was a journey, a journey he longed to see fulfilled. For me it was another chance at life... rebirth and freedom; Redemption would not come easy.

When we crossed the border of Colorado it began to snow. The sun was out; It hadn't been displaced by the clouds. The land was beautiful. Mountains peeked over the horizon reminding me of Switzerland, that place Dad would always describe. It was beyond...

My lips mouthed the words, " Thank you." My tear-filled eyes grazed the blue skies. They were filled with rays of light and hope and wonder. The day I always remember...

In His Arms

By grace I can live and create what is new
By faith I can endure and embrace what I know is true
By dreams I can see the future
By memories I can know my past
By prayers and wishes I can hope to be free, free from it all at last
From all that surrounds me
From all that ever was
From all that they tell me
From all I wish I wasn't
From all whom I have left
From all I look to see
From all that is gone forever
From all that soon will bring
From all the wrongs I have done
From all that has been done to me
Soon my day will come and
With the Lord I'll be
Forever in His arms

In a Dream From that Time

Still I wake on cold, low nights in winter, with snow befalling, in a dream from that time, where so, everything returns. Bitter or sweet, it never matters how, inevitably, it happens. I try to sort through the memories, the forsaken memories. But like wet sands, on cold, worn beaches, the thoughts meld together.

I try to think of an old love, a girlfriend whom I adored, or a tender moment with a friend when we laughed and drank with smiles. I try to find something, anything to hold on to, but the memories are wrong. I know no other word for them. They tear me down until I am left sorrowful and guilty. It's as if they are erased, but still visible somehow, like pencils marks on an old canvas or paper, like colors washed-out by the sun.

And when I visit that old town on the east coast, it's so much worse than a memory. It's as if I in the movie once again, but the boy who once lived is nowhere to be found. He is talked about by family and friends who knew him. His face is captured in pictures, but they are only made of paper. He is like a ghost, but never seems to fade. To those who live there, he is more visible than I. To them I do not exist, except as he in their memories, in their dreams, and in their lives in progress.

Speaking With the Angels

Seven p.m. Tomas, Cortney, Sye and I had all eaten acid. It was a double-sided print; Space ships on one side, stars and stripes on the other. We dosed on two and a half hits each, unaware of the potency of the chemical. We were used of the shit Angel Carson was dealing, that was the problem; His batches were watered down and duplicated for maximum profit.

"Alien blood"-- One of Jones' theories. I snickered to myself. What had become a religion to Jones was not anymore; He had, had a radical conversion. I saw him in the beginning of that night...

I had been waiting for my ride at Charlotte's Web, a local restaurant I had been working for. A car came speeding around the corner with a hub cap flying. At first glance it appeared to be an old police car, but I soon found out it was Kile Jones. He skidded to a screeching halt, and I saw a white object bounce from the driver's seat to the stirring wheel and then back again. I hesitantly approached.

" Jones is that you?" The white object rotated, and underneath I saw a dim silhouette of Kile Jones. " Jones why are you wearing a motorcycle helmet?" " My mother crashed my car that dumb bitch. I'm fucking pissed." The light turned green and Kile Jones sped away. The side of his car was mangled from front to back. That was the night Kile's 'incident.' It turned out he was driving over to Savage Daily's; They had a trip planned for the evening.

We had heard of people having bad trips before, but never knew what was behind it. Kile Jones had become the exception. His only words about that night were, " Do you know what it is to have total faith in God?" Kile Jones was an atheist. I didn't really understand.

By this time, the acid had been kicking in. I sat on one of the dusty sofas in Sye's garage. The last words Cortney had spoken before she went outside were, " It brings me closer to God." Those words circled my brains...

I was falling farther than ever before. I began to see my soul separate from my body. Everything around me became like a pattern, energy. My body was moving like a flower on ocean waves. My hands, weaving through the currents. I noticed a cold sensation on my cheeks-- tears that had been streaming down like rain. I had not blinked; I did not care if I would ever close my eyes again. The air was thick like liquid.

I sent signals to my brain to move my arm, then watched my body move... Like water on glass covering the sun, the trail was thick and thin. I recalled the lyrics of a Pink Floyd tune:

" There's dust in my eyes that blinds my sight, and the silence speaks so much louder than words..."

I had heard Kile Jones explain some things before, whether it was an abstract rendering of truth or literal, I still don't really know. " It's like stopping and smelling the roses," he had said. " The acid permeates every part of you, and forms a thin layer between your brain cells. Your electronic pulses jump between cells, causing a gap in time..."

Timeless space-- where life and death coexist... Where the spirit world and the physical world become one... Where everything remains in being.

And so I entered that place without any warning, and with little knowledge. If it were not for the guardian angels by my side, it would have been my last night on earth.

The digital clock read nine thirty. I watched and waited for it to blink another minute by, but it didn't. I waited even longer; Time, was then still. I began to feel uneasy. There was a familiarity about that place. Like I had been there before and knew somehow that I would return. I was in the womb; I had started here, but I had prematurely returned; I was an intruder. I had broken God given laws. Guilty.

I was terrified-- struggling. My hands and legs were weak. Pink Floyd prophesied on the stereo. " The silence speaks so much louder than words of promises broken." Promises broken... I tried to focus on something else, but my thoughts could not stand in the light of truth. I was dying; I could feel the river of death.

The clock had not changed-- nine thirty still. I sat looking into the physical plane of existence, what I once called reality; Cortney stayed by my side. Cortney turned to me, " Josiah do you want a cigarette?" A distraction, anything, but as I reached my soul was buried deeper. I was not hallucinating; It was real. The life I had been living was the illusion. I could see through it all, the lies, my false self. To you I will not lie!

" Are you sure you don't want a cigarette?" " Yes I'm sure." I could breathe again. Sanity.

Eternity was a near-throw, but by far my last choice. If I were to go any farther, I would have had to check my body at the door. Kile Jones had chosen to. How he had returned was beyond me, but he was not the same. This I knew. Now his words made sense. And all the stories I had heard about people flying off of bridges and buildings did too.

A young man named Cain was at the party. He was possessed inside. Turning and looking at me with eyes ablaze, he mimicked my very words. Words that he had never heard me speak. " Are you trippin dude? How's the trip?" Cold shivers up my spine.

" I have to leave." I got up and started walking. Cain turned to me, " You're going to crash your truck and die." His blatant words, cold like night. Everything stopped around me. Silence, but a heart beat. I sat back down, then conversations resumed.

There was light in Cortney. I could see it in her eyes, but was yet to trust my intuition. I slowly stood to my feet again. Cain turned to me, " Your going to die!" I stopped, though pretended not to listen.

" Besides all of that..." Cortney glistened. " Should we continue?" " Do I have a choice?" She looked over at Cain, her face darkened for a moment. " There's always another choice." " No," I replied. " Please continue."

Tomas sat across the room, an acquaintance I had met through Jones. He looked at me in those moments like he knew exactly what was happening. There was light in him; He was like Cortney, different from the rest. Angels who I trusted.

" It's not my time."

Cortney's eye brows raised. " What do you mean?"

" I love my family... Sarah won't make it without me; She needs me."

" And..."

" And my dad needs my help! He's sick."

I could see the church in my mind: the prayer walk, the green grass, the tall oak trees. That sacred part of me remembered... I saw a picture of a log cabin in fields and mountains in the distance; I had a strange feeling it was to be my home.

Later that night when only Sye and I were left, he took out an aged guitar and began to strum; It's sound was pure. " This is a song I wrote, it's called *Heavens*." Sye closed his eyes, expressionless. I have never forgotten the words.